Wyatt

Wyatt

A Novel by
David Gethin

St. Martin's Press   New York

Library of Congress Cataloging in Publication Data

Gethin, David.
    Wyatt.

    "A Joan Kahn book."
    I. Title.
PR6057.E76W9   1983   823'.914   83-9608
ISBN 0-312-89517-8

First Edition
10 9 8 7 6 5 4 3 2 1

Wyatt

Chapter One

Sir Philip Moresby left No. 10 Downing Street by the rear entrance at a few minutes past ten on a warm August morning. He opened the rear door of a dark green chauffeur-driven Rover and settled himself on the leather upholstery. Laying his silver-topped cane across his briefcase on the seat beside him, he withdrew a solid gold cigarette case from his inside pocket.

"Office, John," he instructed the chauffeur, a small wiry man in dark green uniform who adjusted a pair of dark glasses and eased the car into the street, checking the rearview mirror as he did so.

Thirty yards down the road a second car, with two men in the front, followed Moresby's vehicle. The S.A.S. sergeant in civilian clothes shifted a Browning automatic from a shoulder holster into his right hand.

"In position," he spoke into the car's radio transmitter.

Twenty yards up the road a similar vehicle moved out. A second S.A.S. man, also in civilian clothes, acknowledged the message.

"Clear up front. Alternative Route A," he instructed.

Sir Philip Moresby mentally checked the position of his two escort vehicles and lit his cigarette.

To an inquisitive tourist seeing the smoked glass windows of the dark green car it would seem an important government person were being driven through the Whitehall traffic. The two escorting vehicles would not have merited a second glance. Moresby's car was registered to the Ministry of Defence. The driver was

1

nominally a member of the Civil Service pool of drivers. The escort vehicles did not officially exist.

Sir Philip Moresby was listed in *Who's Who* as a Permanent Secretary to the Ministry, whose clubs were the Athenaeum and the Guards, whose residence was in Portman Square, and whose interests included golf, bridge, backgammon, and archaeology.

He was a member of neither club, lived in Half Moon Street, and had never played a game of golf or bridge in his life. His closest connection with archaeology was having a glass of sherry with the Greek Ambassador. He was an expert at being in places he should not be and never being in places he was expected to be. Since 1942 he had worked in Intelligence and for the past ten years had been the Prime Minister's personal adviser on Intelligence and security matters. He was head of an organization called the Special Services Department. Any member of the House of Commons Public Accounts Committee asking silly questions as to its function was told it was a procurement department for the Ministry of Defence. "Office equipment, files—that sort of thing," as the Defence Minister had once confidently replied.

Special Services Department had a unique function. Both the Secret Intelligence Service (M.I.6) and the Security Service (M.I.5) were subordinate in matters in which S.S.D. chose to concern itself. Sir Philip Moresby therefore outranked "C," head of M.I.6, and the Director General of M.I.5. He was the Prime Minister's eyes, ears, and adviser. Now on his fourth Prime Minister, at the age of sixty-two, he confidently expected to be on a fifth. So whenever he drove to his weekly meeting at 10 Downing Street, he was escorted by the best protection any agency could provide. This was the only occasion Sir Philip Moresby put himself at risk to attack from anyone he or his department had upset—in the highly unlikely event that anyone knew of its existence.

Sir Philip focused his right eye on the minutes of his meeting with the Prime Minister. He had lost the left eye in a raid on Gestapo Headquarters in Paris early in 1944. In its place he wore

2

a grey glass eye indistinguishable in colour from the other. His iron-grey hair, receding slightly, was covered by a bowler hat. The lean face lengthened in puzzlement at some point on which he could not read his own note. His pale complexion was pockmarked around the cheeks, and he was clean-shaven. The pinstripes and coat covered a medium build. The five feet eleven inches carried his 180-pound weight easily, although his stomach was beginning to spread. He kept himself fit by walking long distances on Hampstead Heath on the weekends and by the occasional session in the Ministry gymnasium.

Moresby's car pulled up at the Ministry. This time, John the chauffeur opened Moresby's door, but his eyes were constantly on the street. The watchers in the escort cars scanned the passing faces and vehicles with the darting gaze born of professional protectors. Five minutes later Moresby walked into his top-floor office and the watchers melted into the Whitehall traffic.

Mrs. Burton took coffee into the long, almost Gothic office that was Moresby's inner sanctum. He had settled himself into the vast leather chair that stood behind the enormous mahogany desk. He looked up at her and smiled.

She had been with him twenty years, from the Washington days of C.I.A. liaison through his two years as S.I.S. Eastern European Controller to his present post. Twenty years of putting up with his bad temper, irregular hours, enormous capacity for coffee, and switching arrangements at the last minute had annoyed, exasperated, and, at times, angered her. When she had first worked for him she had been a young widow of twenty-six. Her husband Tom had been in Borneo on counter-insurgency operations when he was killed by a cleverly placed enemy land mine. They had no children and she had soon lost herself in her work. She, like Moresby, had no family ties and had soon made her work her life. Moresby knew there had been someone in Washington, and Mrs. Burton had spent some weeks deciding whether to stay in the States or return to London with Moresby. But Moresby had become a habit. She was married to her job and Moresby was part of that marriage.

There had never been anything physical between them. Moresby looked at her and wondered fleetingly why not. She was an attractive, willowy blond of forty-six whose pale green eyes smiled back at him. He did not even notice her new green dress, let alone comment on it. He eventually spoke the usual greeting.

"Good morning, Dorothy." He took the coffee cup from the desk.

"Good morning, Sir Philip," she replied. The ritual had been the same for twenty years.

"Until an hour ago, I thought it was," he continued. "The P.M. is not happy with the history of S.I.S. Yet another disclosure will be made tomorrow in one of those tabloid newspapers that use words. Its rancid editor fancies seeing his name in the next Honours List so he tipped the P.M. the wink. They are going to blow Hector Runciman. The poor old fool is over eighty and daft as a beanbag. But the masses must be told. I'll never understand why. Everyone knew he was passing low-grade stuff to the Reds when I was a teaboy at Finsbury Circus."

"Not quite true," Dorothy Burton admonished him.

"It was low-grade rubbish," Moresby protested.

"You were never teaboy at the Circus."

"Perhaps not quite. Anyway, the P.M. will be suffering more questions from some idiot of a backbencher out to make a name for himself over events that happened forty years ago. Someone else will say how do we know they're not just as incompetent now. It's egg on face time again, Dorothy. Anyone would think we were the only Intelligence community ever to suffer a couple of defectors and a mole. Talking of moles—is that Czech defector debriefed yet?"

"Alpha says another forty-eight hours. Interim report is on your desk. C.I.A. Head of London Station has invited you to lunch. J.I.C. meeting is at fifteen hundred. C is coming across at twelve hundred to discuss his little problem."

"Excellent. I'll finish my coffee and go for a walk. You did leave me free till twelve?—of course you did."

Moresby settled back in his chair to read Alpha's interim report on the Czech defector. As usual the defector was complaining that no notice had been taken of his early disclosures. Moresby had soon digested the salient points, but one sentence had him puzzled for a moment. He lifted an internal telephone and spoke.

"Alpha. Are you sure this report is an accurate transcript?"

"Eyes only head of S.S.D., sir. I typed it myself from my own recorded conversation. We are the only parties with knowledge of its contents."

"Thank you, Alpha."

Moresby replaced the receiver and walked over to the window. He looked through the bulletproof glass toward St. James' Park. He had fifteen minutes to make the meet.

There was a twinge in the pit of his stomach and his mouth felt dry. He put the feeling down to too many cigarettes that morning. From a locked desk drawer he took a small sealed plain brown envelope, which he slipped into his inside jacket pocket. Taking the bowler hat and silver-topped cane, he strode from his office.

He walked across Horse Guards Parade and into St. James' Park. Fleetingly he wondered why everyone in his business met in parks. He felt uneasy, nervous even. Maybe he had been too long out of active operations. Yet his streetcraft still functioned. There was no sign of a tail, but the twinge was back in the pit of his stomach. His mouth felt dry. He began to feel hot and not because of the August sun beating down from an almost cloudless sky. Was he suffering from funk? Mission twitch, the youngsters called it now. He cast his mind back over the years to the past operations. No, he had always felt this way, just before a meet. Today's meet was the most unorthodox and perhaps the most important of all.

He observed the passersby, casually but very carefully—secretaries hurrying to an office, a family of Dutch tourists, the middle-aged lady walking a dachshund. A group of students passed him, animatedly discussing something. The fashions amused him, bright, glaring colours. To be young again, he reflected. Not really, he decided. Then he saw the Libyan, a hundred yards away, occupying a bench by the lakeside, gazing toward the ever-changing London skyline.

Moresby walked on, resisting the temptation to quicken the

pace. He had ten yards to go but the Libyan gave no indication of having seen him, although Moresby knew he had. Casually Moresby sat on the bench next to the Libyan, but not too close. The Libyan looked across at him.

"Good morning." Morseby smiled, unfolded his *Times*, and began to read.

The Libyan nodded and went back to watching the skyline. He was a tall man, over six feet, with penetrating blue eyes hidden by dark glasses. His thin upper lip was disguised by a small dark moustache. He smoked a thin cigar, flicking the ash aimlessly onto the pathway. His lightweight suit and silk shirt were from expensive London makers. The thin fingers of his hands were adorned with rings.

After some minutes the Libyan smiled a thin smile and, sneering, withdrew an envelope from his inside jacket pocket. As he did so, Moresby casually moved his silver-topped cane to his right hand, stood up, and held the now folded *Times* in his left hand. He walked past the Libyan, carelessly dropping the newspaper onto the man's lap.

"I'm ever so sorry," Moresby apologized.

"Not at all," the Libyan replied, retrieving the paper and handing it to Moresby, who walked back the way he had come.

Inside the folded newspaper was the envelope the Libyan had withdrawn from his pocket. And the Libyan now possessed the envelope Moresby had taken from the desk.

As he crossed the park, Moresby spotted a short, athletically built man in a track suit who appeared to be jogging too slowly for his weight and age. Moresby's grip tightened on his silver-topped cane but he gave no indication of his awareness. The man passed Moresby and ran off to his left.

"Mission twitch." Moresby laughed to himself.

Chapter Two

Sir Philip Moresby was back at the Ministry of Defence by ten to twelve. He walked through the outer office where Mrs. Burton was typing. She looked up at him as if to say something important, then looked down at the typewriter again. He wondered, momentarily, whether she usually pounded typewriter keys that hard. As he opened his own door an instinct born of years, awakened by Mrs. Burton's behaviour, told him something was wrong. An instant later he knew it.

Two men stood in his office, one by his desk and the other by the window. No one was allowed to enter Moresby's inner office unless he himself was present. He started to say something but the man at his desk interrupted in a cold, unfriendly voice. Very strange, because he and M.I.5's Director of Operations had been on friendly terms for years.

"Sorry about the intrusion, Philip, but we have a problem."

Moresby was about to suggest it had better be a serious one for even Richard Lansbury to invade his inner sanctum, but he stopped himself and read the look on Lansbury's lined and mournful face, which always reminded him of a sulky spaniel. His usually soft brown eyes were hostile, and his broad shoulders were covered by a light mackintosh with epaulettes. Lansbury seldom went out on the streets these days, but when he did, whatever the weather, he wore the light mackintosh.

Lansbury lit his old briar pipe and glanced at the second man as if giving some kind of signal.

"Calladyne here has some points to raise with you."

Moresby had never seen or heard of Calladyne before. There was no reason he should have. Of medium height and stocky build, Calladyne gave the impression of being an athlete. The blond hair was cropped to the skull. His cold grey eyes fixed Moresby with a neutral stare. Hands were held low in front of him. The green double-breasted blazer was open. An old Etonian tie was, thought Moresby, slightly out of place on a man who was in his late twenties. The lines and broken nose suggested some years of experience in the more physical side of life.

"Sir Philip. About thirty minutes ago you met a man in St. James' Park."

The voice was flat, toneless. The accent was very Eton.

"You then exchanged packages with him. In the package you gave him was a memorandum of discussions between Heads of Cairo Station S.I.S. and C.I.A. I would be interested to see what is in the package he gave you."

Now, for the first time, Moresby spoke.

"I don't know what you've been playing at, sonny, or how you know the contents of that package."

"We've detained the gentleman, a Libyan. Colonel Abdul Fahd, head of the People's Foreign Intelligence Section."

Moresby looked angrily at Richard Lansbury.

"Did you authorize this, Dick?"

Calladyne cut in before Lansbury could reply.

"This operation has authorization. Head of Cairo Station S.I.S. was involved in a fatal car accident only this morning."

"Doubtless C will inform me in due course."

"Not to put too fine a point on it, Philip, Calladyne here thinks you've been at it." Lansbury puffed philosophically on his pipe.

"He has authorization, so let's have a look at your envelope, shall we?"

Moresby's brain raced. Something had gone seriously wrong. They knew what was in his envelope, otherwise Lansbury's attitude would be very different. And this public school thug would be standing very smartly to attention when addressing the head of S.S.D. Mrs. Burton's behaviour had been caused by a conflict of loyalties.

"Certainly." Moresby tossed the envelope onto the desk. Calladyne crossed in front of him and opened the envelope. It was bulky. Moresby had expected that. But he had not expected the bulk to contain one hundred fifty pound notes.

"Running expenses, Sir Philip?" Calladyne inquired smugly.

Moresby resisted an impulse to raise the silver-topped cane he still held and let Calladyne have a .38 Special hollow-point bullet where it hurt.

Lansbury said, "Calladyne had you tailed all the way, observed and photographed."

"The man in the track suit." Moresby shook his head.

"And the girl in the running shorts."

"I didn't notice her."

"Philip, you must be getting old. She even had my old blood pressure rising there for a while. Give young Calladyne his due. He only put on a four-man tail. You fell for it all the way. And that exchange—the old newspaper routine. Still, maybe it's so old as to be original."

Moresby sat down at his desk. The twinge in the pit of his stomach was now a sickening pain. The Libyan had set him up. But there was more—there had to be. He felt angry and amazed—angry that he was being treated this way, that he had not covered himself—amazed this was happening to him.

"I have a very reasonable explanation," Moresby replied.

"Doubtless, Sir Philip." Calladyne nodded. "Which will take into account the death of S.I.S. Cairo Head of Station and explain the money in this envelope. It will explain a recent thirty-thousand-pound deposit in your bank at Harrow and why you were passing top-secret information to the Libyans. It may explain the loss of seven agents when you were S.I.S. Head of Eastern European section and the nasty business in Algeria back in fifty-eight. There was the Budapest mess in forty-nine. How many spanners did you plant in the Gehlen Org Works when you reorganized German Intelligence participation?"

"So you see, Philip," Lansbury cut in. "No wonder the Krauts didn't know whether they were on their arses or their elbows over Brandt."

"That's enough, Dick." Moresby reached for his telephone. "I'm calling the P.M."

"P.M. already knows, old boy. Don't think I'd be waltzing in here like some flat-footed noddy unless this operation had political backup, do you? Otherwise you'd have our guts for the proverbial honi soit qui mal. In the words of Calladyne's less sophisticated chums down at Horseferry House, you're nicked, Philip. Sorry, old boy." Lansbury held the office door open.

Calladyne took Moresby's coat. They walked through Mrs. Burton's office. A red-headed girl with exquisite shoulders wearing a running vest and shorts was sitting next to Mrs. Burton, long legs dangling over the desk. Mrs. Burton looked up at Moresby. He could have sworn he saw tears in her eyes.

"Don't flap, Dorothy." He smiled. "Five have put their size nines in it again."

The girl picked up a telephone and gave a string of instructions. Lansbury was right. She did make your blood pressure rise.

They drove from the Ministry in two cars. Lansbury and Calladyne accompanied Moresby. The girl followed with Mrs. Burton in the second car. This time there was no chauffeur called John and no S.A.S. escort. As they drove through the London traffic Moresby's mind went back forty years to the days of the Special Operations Executive and the agent training he had received. He was now in a position where his cover had been blown; capture had been effected. Interrogation was the next ordeal.

He wondered how £30,000 had found its way into a bank account at Harrow in his name. The account was his, opened by him on a whim three years before when he had won £1,000 on the Premium Bonds and decided to keep the money in a separate branch of a separate bank from his main account. Someone had researched this project very well. Every operation that had ever gone wrong was now being credited to his treachery. Someone had fingered him, poisoned the atmosphere. Soon he would be removed. To whose advantage? He started with the Libyans.

They had ties with every terrorist group operating in Europe. Libya trained the I.R.A., Black June, Bader-Meinhof, Red Brigade—any Mickey Mouse outfit that raised the price of a phone call to the local People's Bureau. Any Eastern-bloc Intelligence would be happy with his demise. Moscow Centre would be delighted—and they had the capability. Elements in M.I.5 and M.I.6 would like to see a change. The C.I.A. were not his best friends, not since the previous London Station chief had started a stupid, uncontrolled drug experiment on some unsuspecting guinea pigs of British university students. Moresby's reaction had put a considerable strain on the special relationship.

The thoughts raced around his brain. He tried to distil motives, opportunity, results—unsuccessfully. He needed more information. He hoped he could get Lansbury on his own. Dick had not enjoyed the interview; Calladyne had. A suitably cold and nasty young man, that. Gratuitous. Not Lansbury's usual style of operator. Lansbury had seemed to be present to lend weight and prestige to the interview. Calladyne had done most of the talking and the accusing.

Feelings of unreality, of dreamlike awareness, came over Moresby as he was led into an interrogation room. A large, aggressive person in dark blue uniform emptied his pockets, took his jacket, tie, shoelaces, watch, and even his handkerchief. Moresby was pushed toward a wooden chair secured under a bright pool of white light. A door banged and he heard bolts being slammed into place.

The room was sixty feet by fifteen, walls and ceiling painted white to cause a disorientation. Bare of furniture except for the single chair, the desired effect was easily achieved—to make a suspect feel he was the only thing in the room, the sole object of the white uniform terror that climbed the cold walls to the flat ceiling relieved only by a circle of bright light encased in a metal grille.

Moresby knew the technique.

The suspect was initially left alone. The first fifteen minutes made you realize you had nothing to focus your attention on, nothing to fiddle with, nothing to look at. The room was uncertainty—what was happening outside was uncertainty. From the uncertainty came doubts, apprehension. Were your family and friends safe? Had they been taken? If not, had they been told? When you did not arrive home, what would they do? How long had you been there? Then the fears set in. You lost track of time, of tangible things. You felt alone and cold. When would someone come? What would they do? Finally, minutes, hours, or was it days later, came the businesslike arrival of the interrogators, shuffling their papers, exchanging knowing glances. The "come on now—you didn't mean to do it—we know how you feel— make it easy on yourself" routine.

The only foolproof method of proving an espionage case was a confession. Moresby had obtained several in his time. His usual method was the endless conversations between himself and the suspect, spread over days in a congenial office atmosphere. Occasionally he had to resort to rougher means. Somehow the bright lights and disorientation weren't Lansbury's methods.

"I'm sorry, Calladyne," Moresby spoke out loud, knowing the microphone concealed somewhere in the ceiling would pick his voice up. Moresby knew he was on closed-circuit television, but did not make a useless attempt to locate the camera.

"It won't do. If you've read the reports you'll know the Gestapo once had me for forty-eight hours. I'd suggest the old sodium pentothal routine. Then I can have a nice cup of tea and lie down."

He crossed to the chair, sat down, and stretched his legs.

In a large office along the stone corridor, Calladyne, Lansbury, and the girl sat sipping coffee and watching a television screen showing Moresby's cell. A bank of telephones was arranged on a table against the wall. In one corner stood a large cocktail cabinet, in the other a computer screen and console.

"Didn't take him long to work out it was your operation, did it, Calladyne?"

"No, sir," Calladyne replied.

"Well, you've both heard the suspect's advice, his first words for two hours," Lansbury continued. "Now children, listen to this and learn from it. Then I shall leave you and report to Mr. Quittenden. By the way, he's instructed me to tell you that as from now you're on secondment to his section."

Calladyne smiled to himself. Lansbury caught the expression and knew that someone was definitely playing office politics. Quittenden had ordered Lansbury to release Calladyne and the girl, Vicky Keane. Quittenden had no right to give such an order. When Lansbury had questioned it, Quittenden had become abrupt and suggested that Lansbury do as he was told. The tone of voice told Lansbury that Quittenden had the pull to do whatever he wanted.

"Sir Philip Moresby is an unprincipled, devious, cunning, brave old bastard who's been in this business forty years. He's sent a few operatives over the top to certain death and he's led from the front on more than one occasion—in the line of duty outside whatever else he might have done. He's shrewd and twenty years ago, Calladyne, he'd have tied you in judo knots and used you for a football. So don't go at him with the smug 'I'm going to nail you' attitude. And you stop smirking, Vicky, my darling. He's not some old has-been. He'd still screw your arse off and leave you wondering where he learnt it all. Which reminds me, go and put some clothes on and bring that recording of your little chat with Mrs. Burton. I believe she's clean but I've been instructed to warn her about talking to anyone."

He watched the girl leave the office and turned to the cocktail cabinet.

"Lovely rear end on that, Calladyne. You giving it one?"

The young man shook his head and noted Lansbury did not offer him a whisky. Calladyne wished his boss would leave the earthy humour at home.

"Not your cup of tea. Not gay, are you? 'Course not. I've read the reports. Word of advice, lad, about Moresby. I know it's Quittenden's job now and I can't think why. But no rough stuff, and have a doctor look at him every four hours, just to cover yourself, eh?''

"As you said, sir, it's Mr. Quittenden's job now."

Lansbury put down the whisky glass, picked up his coat, and opened the office door. Vicky Keane came in holding a typed report and two cassettes.

"Thank you, Vicky, my darling." He slapped the girl's bottom, which was now encased in tight blue jeans.

"Be good, children." He leered as he closed the door behind him.

Vicky Keane and Calladyne exchanged glances.

"Goodbye, Dirty Dick, and thank you." Calladyne gave a two-fingered gesture to the door. "Doesn't he become very boring?"

"That's the third time he's slapped my arse today. Is he all talk?"

Calladyne nodded.

"About women, yes. The real stuff—no way. Now we'll go and talk to Sir Philip. Do you think Mrs. Burton is clean?"

"Dirty Dick is right. She's clean. She may be close to Moresby but she's married to the service first. Moresby is just a fantasy lover and she knows it."

"Very psychological."

"I did the course, remember."

Chapter Three

R ichard Lansbury was summoned to the Director General of
M.I.5's private office on his return from the Finchley interrogation centre. He was invited to sit down and given a large
glass of single-malt whisky. The Director General introduced
him to a portly, bespectacled Welshman named Gareth Llewellyn
Jones.

"L.J. and I have just come from the Prime Minister,
Lansbury."

He had heard of Llewellyn Jones before, but had never met the
man. Lansbury thought he was a Permanent Secretary to the
Home Office. The Director General had not divulged the man's
precise function.

Gareth Llewellyn Jones' immaculately pinstriped exterior concealed a soul of pure selfishness. The dark, bushy hair covered a
highly sophisticated and devious brain. He had spent fifty years
trying to lose the accent of his birthplace and had very nearly
succeeded. The last thirty of those fifty years had been spent in
the pursuit and acquisition of departmental power. He was now a
familiar figure in the decision-making process, very close to the
Prime Minister and unpopular with a certain section of the Cabinet, who referred to him as "that unspeakable Welsh Richelieu."
Others had dubbed him a "counterfeit Lloyd George." To his
subordinates he was "that little bastard"—a slur on his parents,
both highly respected Methodist businesspeople in what had once
been a small Welsh steel town.

In direct contrast, the D.G. of Five was a fifty-three-year-old patrician, Eton and Balliol, second son of nobility whose life had been spent in aesthetic pleasures, a successful career in the Army, and later diplomacy. His face was tanned, clean shaven with a pleasant open smile and bright blue eyes. Brown hair was greying around the temples. The pianist's fingers of his right hand drummed on the desk. Lansbury liked him, could work with him, respected him as a good, honourable man, but did not think much of his executive ability.

"The Prime Minister, Lansbury, is naturally apoplectic; so are the other privileged few that know," Llewellyn Jones began. "I understand from Quittenden you were reluctant to release two of your agents to his department."

Lansbury caught the warning glance his D.G. shot him, but ignored it.

"Mr. Quittenden is a high-ranking S.I.S. officer, sir, but he has no jurisdiction over my agents."

Llewellyn Jones smiled.

"I understand the strict departmental separation, Lansbury. However, if Mr. Quittenden asks for the moon, you give it to him. Do you understand?"

"Yes, sir."

"This government, not to say this country, is faced with the appalling prospect that its Intelligence supremo is a traitor. The damage done is incomprehensible, the repercussions inconceivable. Mr. Quittenden has been personally selected, by those who decide these matters, to take charge of the entire business. He has every facility and resource available to him and every authority to act. You will report to him and take instructions on a need-to-know basis. Is that clear?"

"Perfectly, sir."

"Thank you, Lansbury."

The interview was obviously over. Lansbury hastily finished his whisky and left.

Once in his own office, he poured himself another large one to recover from the shell shock of the day's events and Llewellyn Jones' ruthless verbal barrage. He had been ordered to report to

Quittenden but Quittenden could bloody well wait until he'd finished his scotch.

He knew of Simon Quittenden, and had spoken to him briefly at an interdepartmental meeting. That and the telephone conversation earlier in the day were the only contacts he had ever made. But he did not breathe the same air as the exalted circles of S.I.S. where Quittenden was No. 3. Many people tipped him to go right to the top. He was reputed to be tough, shrewd, devious, and unprincipled—just like Sir Philip Moresby.

"How are the mighty fallen," Llewellyn Jones observed, following Lansbury's departure.

"Sorry," the D.G. apologized. "Didn't quite catch that."

"Sir Philip Moresby, and to a certain extent, Lansbury. Quittenden only wants him as an office boy, to do the legwork. Says he's too much in with Moresby."

"Hard to believe it of Moresby, L.J. I didn't think the man had an ounce of disloyalty in him. Devious, yes. Traitorous, never. Still, just shows in this game, doesn't it? Any idea who'll succeed him?"

"I have," Llewellyn Jones replied. "Who would your choice be?"

"An outsider, I think. Someone who isn't tainted with the aroma of the whole wretched Intelligence business. These appalling disclosures in the press. Now we find a second-generation super-Philby. God knows what damage has been done. I would be inclined to an outsider—yourself, for instance."

Llewellyn Jones waved his hand in mock dismissal.

"You're in the running, of course. But to avoid any disappointment, I'll be frank with you."

"You usually are, L.J."

"The P.M. favours Quittenden."

The D.G. reflected for a moment.

"Right away from the Oxbridge style, eh? Redbrick, practical man. Good choice—superb planner, excellent staff officer, and a good politician. He'd do a far better job than I would."

"Must take my leave, Charles. Keep all this under your hat. Need to know, I think you fellows say."

Simon Quittenden looked younger than his forty-five years. He worked intensively and long. He had no time for a family—resulting in the breakup of his marriage ten years previously. His wealthy and attractive wife had remarried. Quittenden had forgotten what she looked like and now had difficulty remembering the children's names. Long ago he had ceased to remember birthdays. In turn, they had forgotten him and now called their stepfather "Dad," which did not bother Quittenden unduly.

To everyone in S.I.S. he was known simply as "Q," not a code name but a sobriquet. No one had been able to invent anything more amusing, slanderous, or rude. He was a man who caused neutral personal feelings in those around him. The son of a bank manager, he had attended Grammar School, the L.S.E., and later Harvard Law School on an English Speaking Union scholarship. Recruited into S.I.S. as an organizer, Quittenden was a manipulator, a compulsive intriguer with himself. Possessed of a hard, brilliant, unemotional mind, his natural stablemates were the Llewellyn Joneses, the career power-seekers. He despised the bluff professionals like Lansbury, to whom he referred as "that provincial buffoon," and he pitied the time-servers only for as long as it took him to elbow them from his upward path.

Quittenden had worked his way up the S.I.S. ladder organizing one department after another. The C.I.A., regarding him as the management consultant of S.I.S., looked on as heads started rolling and inefficiency and waste were cut from the body intelligent.

Quittenden's sources of information were second to none. In a world where exchanged information was stock-in-trade, he was master of one-way traffic. He received all and gave little or nothing concrete in return. There were vague hints that favours done would be remembered, his not-inconsiderable influence used. Invariably he managed to be seen to act. But the outcome was favourable to one cause—his own.

He had known Moresby was meeting the Libyan. Ten days previously a chance remark by a lowly M.I.5 case officer whose duty it was to target Arab Intelligence units in the U.K. had told Quittenden that Moresby had seen Fahd on two previous occasions. He had even received reports on Fahd's movements and transcripts of telephone calls. All this on an unofficial "if I can do you a favour some time" basis. He also knew that someone in M.I.5 had reported Moresby's activities to the Permanent Secretary, Llewellyn Jones, and thence to the Cabinet Office. He was aware that since the previous Thursday, Richard Lansbury had been ordered to check on the allegations.

So when Llewellyn Jones had summoned Quittenden to a meeting at eleven-thirty on Sunday morning, Q was not unduly surprised. Q, with approval from No. 10, had been given the task of controlling the operation to catch and take Moresby. Llewellyn Jones did not tell Q he would succeed Moresby. Jungle instinct had given Q the scent months before. He wanted the job. He needed to be Head of S.S.D., to hold power, to have the ultimate influence.

He reflected on the irony. Execute your predecessor, then put your head on the block he has vacated. The thought amused him. The possibility of Moresby's innocence was immaterial to him. The prima facie case was strong. In the unlikely event that Moresby's innocence was proved, Quittenden would recommend that his laxity in putting himself in such a position left Moresby unfit to retain the post he held.

Quittenden checked his watch. 1715. He pressed a desk intercom.

"Send Lansbury in." The voice was toneless.

Quittenden could smell the tobacco a full ten seconds before Lansbury entered, puffing his briar.

"Do sit down," Quittenden invited. To Lansbury the words sounded more like a threat.

Lansbury looked around the Lancaster Gate office.

The lighting was flourescent, bathing the entire room in an almost unreal white light. Apart from the steel desk and leather chair, the furnishings looked like a science fiction filmset gone berserk. There were none of the dusty filing cabinets, potted plants, Victorian armchairs, or reproduction cocktail cabinets he usually associated with M.I.6. Instead, on one wall of the office, was a bank of data screens and electronic equipment—a word processor, computer terminals, closed-circuit television, audio-visual communications links to M.I.6's operations room. As he watched, a screen flickered and he recognized the interior of his own operations room at M.I.5. In one corner of the room was a camp bed, at the foot of which stood a four-tiered circular table bearing a coffee percolater, mill, sugar, and cups. The second tier was a chess board with pieces in futuristic black and white design. On the third tier: a box of cigarettes, lighter, and various spirit bottles. On the last tier was a boxlike electronic gadget Lansbury had never seen.

"How the self-contained robot lives," Lansbury whispered to himself, then to Quittenden:

"I'm reporting as instructed."

He looked hard at Quittenden and did not like what he saw. A man in his forties with short fair hair. Six feet, lean and athletic, dressed like an American business executive. The face was neither antagonistic nor friendly, but the eyes seemed to change from brown to green and back again. Or was it his imagination? Quittenden lit a cigarette and eased himself into the chair. Lansbury's chair was halfway down the office. He felt intimidated by its position facing Quittenden. Behind him was a black wall.

"You've seen Llewellyn Jones. He's told you I'm running this operation."

Smug bastard, thought Lansbury. "Yes, sir."

"What have you got so far?"

"I thought Calladyne was reporting to you."

"He is. I'd like your report."

"According to your instructions, using a four-man tail, we observed and photographed Sir Philip Moresby meeting Abdul Fahd this morning. We arrested both. Sir Philip and his secretary were taken to Finchley. The Libyans sent a representative to the F.C.O. within the hour. We were advised to release Fahd, who has since been packed off to Tripoli with the diplomatic bag. He only knew four words of English—I am a diplomat.''

"Your impressions?"

"I think Mrs. Burton is in the clear. I think Moresby was operating on his own for legitimate reasons. Someone cleared Fahd out of here damned quick. And I wouldn't trust the Libyans as far as I could throw the People's Bureau.''

"Reasons?"

"I listened to Mrs. Burton's interrogation. I've known Moresby twenty years. And who'd trust the Libyans?"

"Emotional rather than rational," Q observed.

Lansbury studied the strong, tanned features. His policeman's gaze took in the strong yet graceful hands, the two gold rings. There was a hint of expensive after-shave. Here was a man you expected to pop up in a menswear advertisement for action clothes that turned women wild. He also looked like a man who'd go for three rounds with a professional boxer and dance his way out of trouble before finishing the bout with a totally unexpected kick to the groin followed by a karate blow.

Lansbury definitely did not like Quittenden very much. Moresby he respected, feared a little, but liked. The D.G. was all right in his own way. Llewellyn Jones' political authority and Machiavellian style made him nervous. But Quittenden's almost schizophrenic presence scared the hell out of him. The fellow looked like a clean-living, well-manicured ladies' man. He talked like a computer playing chess with itself.

"My methods have worked in the past," Lansbury defended himself. He could see young Calladyne in this man. Or was it the other way round?

"Fahd was targetted by your department," Quittenden stated. "Were you advised Moresby met him on two previous occasions?"

The crunch question, thought Lansbury. Where the hell does

he get his information? Lansbury knew of the meetings. Moresby had casually mentioned the fact to him. Technically, Lansbury should have advised his superior. But Moresby could go anywhere, do anything.

"I was aware of the fact."

"And you did nothing, took no action?"

"Moresby mentioned it to me, that he had seen Fahd."

"Before or after your people advised you?"

Now I'm on the hit list, Lansbury thought. He mentally wrestled with his response for a second or two. The truth would look bad for Moresby, a lie could be fatal for him. Quittenden had the knives out.

"I think it may have been after."

"Loyalty to your friends might be creditable at Eton. Not in this business," Quittenden replied.

"I left secondary school at sixteen," Lansbury quipped. He knew it was a poor response, but the best he could think up.

"It was after," Quittenden continued, stubbing his cigarette out.

Then why ask? You bastard, Lansbury thought.

"That's why Calladyne controlled the observation and Moresby's arrest?" Lansbury demanded.

"Partially. When I run an operation, I decide the personnel irrespective of whose job it is to do what. The problem when dealing with an Establishment figure who's gone bent is that you chaps in Five seem to refuse to believe the evidence. This is why I'm controlling this operation."

"If you say so," Lansbury countered.

"Rational, not emotional. The options are clear. Either Moresby has been set up, or he is guilty. He knew you were targetting Fahd. So he casually mentions to you they've met—after he knows he's been spotted. He uses his position to bluff his way out. Who is going to dare suspect him? He's off on his omnipotent course, doing what he wants to, whenever, because he is head of S.S.D. He knows that if he drops the Libyan even you will become suspicious, so he carries on. That means guilty to me. A set up by the Libyans or anyone else would have entailed broader clues, a tipoff to you or to us.''

Quittenden rose from his chair, lighting another cigarette. He walked to the curtained window and back again before continuing.

"Why do people spy? Idealism, money, romance, adventure, concealment of past misdeeds or vice. There are no past misdeeds in Moresby's life other than occupational service hazards. He has no family. His vices are infrequent and aboveboard. At sixty-two, he's seen enough adventure. Idealism. I'm looking into the Balliol period 1936–39, and that may prove fruitful. Money—he has a bank account at Harrow where money has been paid in on a regular basis over the past six months. Paying-in slips are signed by a P.H. Moresby. There is little doubt the signatures are his. Over twenty-five thousand pounds has been paid in during that period. Money and idealism, Lansbury. Two good reasons.''

"What does Moresby say to this?'' Lansbury asked.

"Nothing at all. Refuses to comment. I've not yet used any interrogation methods other than conversation.''

"What am I doing now?'' Lansbury demanded.

"Stand by to locate his escape route.''

Lansbury raised his eyebrows.

"Someone will either offer to exchange him, or they'll actively try and spring him. I don't believe he'll be left to rot. Moscow Centre look after their own. Of course he's working for the Centre. You will take a small unit and stand by at Finchley tomorrow morning. Moresby has asked for a lawyer. I'm going to let him have one. He may try and arrange his escape through an intermediary. Do you get my picture?''

"Definitely,'' Lansbury replied.

Lansbury was glad of the fresh air as he walked to his car. Monday, August 23, had seen the security world turned upside down. The inferences were clear. He had better impress the new order or Quittenden would ensure that M.I.5 had a new director of operations.

Chapter Four

Tuesday, August 24, was another fine, hot day. Sir Philip Moresby watched the dawn break at the Finchley interrogation centre. He had been taken to more comfortable quarters the previous evening. Admittedly, the window was barred, but the bedroom was well furnished, the bookcase full, and hot water in the adjoining bathroom plentiful.

Quittenden had spent the evening with him, talking, mainly to himself because Moresby had refused to discuss anything more controversial than the Australian cricket team. Quittenden had been annoyed, coldly hostile at times. At others, the man had been affable—well, as affable as Quittenden could ever be. But he had achieved the purpose of his visit—to implant in Moresby's mind the doubt that there would be no trial, no escape, only an unpleasant accident.

Which worried Moresby. He was not afraid of dying—only of dying before his purpose had been accomplished. He had found sleep difficult and knew that had been Quittenden's intention. Lack of sleep meant lowering mental defences. Mistakes then occurred. Moresby knew that mistakes would lead to the unpleasant accident. Quittenden had used the threat to induce Moresby to talk. Moresby was one step ahead. He knew that if he talked, the threat would be executed. If he kept silent, Quittenden would only bluff.

Unknown to Moresby, there had been little sleep for S.I.S. that night. Their agent Bennett had been arrested by the K.G.B. at five minutes past one that morning. The news hit S.I.S. operations room at four-thirty. Quittenden's instant electronics advised him immediately. He telephoned Gareth Llewellyn Jones and C, Head of M.I.6, at five twenty-five. The news was given to a sleepy Prime Minister at 6:00 A.M. A breakfast meeting was scheduled at Downing Street for 8:30 A.M. Llewellyn Jones and Quittenden attended. Information, although sketchy, was collated, and papers on various options were prepared at once.

The K.G.B. staff at the London Embassy worked swiftly. Their first call to the F.C.O. was in by 8:40 A.M. An urgent matter for immediate discussion had arisen. Broad hints were being dropped: "We have something you want" and vice versa. The news reached Downing Street as the security meeting convened, fifteen minutes late. Lansbury was contacted by scrambler telephone. Llewellyn Jones was furious at the response.

"We've no one to exchange unless you want me to lift a couple of bookies' runners," Lansbury admitted, then ventured an opinion that did nothing to assuage Llewellyn Jones' anger.

"Do you think we've got something they want?"

Which resulted in the telephone being slammed down on him.

"This may indicate Moresby is their man. And they don't want us to try him," the Prime Minister observed acidly.

"Assuming they ask for Moresby," Llewellyn Jones replied, more in hope than expectation.

"Tit for tat," Quittenden remarked. "Moresby was lifted at eleven-thirty yesterday. Just over twelve hours later they grab our best-placed agent their side of the Curtain. Insurance job."

"How important is Bennett?" Llewellyn Jones demanded.

"Don't ask," Quittenden replied. "Six years' work and a network of twenty agents blown. He'll never hold out."

"What a price to pay." The P.J. silently contemplated the coffee.

"Was your snatch operation on Moresby observed?" Llewellyn Jones asked.

"If I were Moscow Centre I'd cover my man. I'd certainly watch those Libyan hooligans as a matter of course," Quittenden replied.

"Even if they were working with you?"

"Prime Minister, especially if they were working with me."

"Recommendations, gentlemen."

"Exchange," Llewellyn Jones replied.

Both he and the Prime Minister looked at Quittenden. The Prime Minister spoke.

"You're my security adviser, Q."

Quittenden did three seconds' work to hide a spark of vanity. But his answer was prepared.

"Do not rule out the possibility of an exchange. But we can stall Centre for days, even weeks. Moresby probably has an alternative escape route. We let him make contact. Irrespective of what we do, Centre has got Bennett and through him one of our networks. We observe Moresby's contacts and see if they use a Centre network we can destroy. Then I suggest Moresby could be exchanged for Bennett, or he could be tried, or—" Quittenden paused for a moment as though justifying an unpleasant decision to himself, "he could have an unfortunate accident. It will save the political embarrassment of a criminal trial."

Llewellyn Jones smiled to himself. The Prime Minister was silent for a moment, then coughed.

"Very frank advice, Q. But I think that we should stop wishing accidents on people actively. For the moment at least."

Sir Philip Moresby was moved to a safe house in Norwood at 9:35 A.M. for a meeting with his solicitor.

Sir Nigel Appleton was senior partner in the firm of Stansgate Appleton, a corporate partnership as respected as the Inns of Court and as diverse as the law itself. On receipt of Moresby's message, Appleton had cancelled all appointments for that morning and was driven to Norwood in his Rolls-Royce Silver Shadow.

Moresby looked on with some relief as the heavy, bespectacled Sir Nigel eased his short, corpulent frame into an armchair. Appleton looked around the comfortably furnished drawing room and gratefully accepted a dry sherry brought by a thin man wearing sports trousers and open-necked shirt, who left the decanter on a coffee table. Moresby lit his own cigarette and explained the events of the day before to Appleton, who listened attentively and jotted an occasional note on a small pad. Eventually he walked to the window and looked out.

"I sincerely hope this conversation is not being overheard, Philip. There is a prima facie case against you. The documents you passed—their contents and value are a matter of evidence. But the money in that bank account is difficult."

"So what do I do?" Moresby asked.

"Absolutely nothing. They'll probably hold you under Prevention of Terrorism or something suitable for a week. They may even try and stretch it before charging you. I can always apply for habeus corpus in that instance, but don't worry. If I were you I'd take the opportunity to catch up on some reading. The sherry is bearable. Food all right? You can see me whenever you want—I don't see any difficulty there. If there is, I shall take steps, so sit tight. Let's see their evidence."

Moresby motioned to Appleton, who gave him the notepad. Moresby started writing on it. After some minutes, Appleton took the notepad and puzzled for a moment at the written instructions. But he said nothing and left the room.

Appleton's Rolls-Royce Silver Shadow had been followed to its destination by a twelve-man surveillance team working in relays under the field command of Richard Lansbury. Telephone surveillance was set up on the offices of Stansgate Appleton. Directional finding radio equipment vans appeared in the street outside disguised as service vehicles investigating culverts. By the time Sir Nigel Appleton walked to lunch carrying the same briefcase he had carried to the interview with Sir Philip Moresby, an eight-man tail was covering his every footstep. By the time he sat down to his consommé with a lunch guest, a transcript of his meeting with Moresby was on Quittenden's desk.

Llewellyn Jones read his copy over lunch at his club. He had already met a Soviet diplomat at the F.C.O. who had more than hinted at a proposal to exchange Sir Philip Moresby for the S.I.S.

agent Bennett. Llewellyn Jones had not denied the possibility of an exchange but had made discouraging noises and denied knowledge of anyone called Bennett. He was playing for time. Quittenden wanted to see where Moresby's contacts led. Bennett was left to the psychological mercy of Moscow Centre's hallucinogenic drugs.

Chapter Five

David Lewis was sitting in the bar of Romulus, an extremely expensive and discreet restaurant deep in the City, by 12:45 P.M. on Tuesday. He had been invited to meet Sir Nigel Appleton for lunch.

Lewis had put on a new dark pinstripe suit that morning before catching the 8:30 A.M. 125 from Pontowyn, a busy little market and county town in West Wales where all his legal work was done. He had risen early and spoken to his fourteen-year-old daughter about what she wanted him to bring her back from London. He knew what to buy his wife. He was not sure about his secretary's present. She had wanted to accompany him on the London trip, but he had firmly refused. He was to meet the celebrated Sir Nigel Appleton, and the chance of impressing a contact in such exalted legal circles was too good to have his potential mistress seen in such circumstances. London solicitors might take their secretaries to meetings, provincial Welsh solicitors did not.

Lewis sipped his sherry. He was happier with beer, but the surroundings and his appointment dictated sherry. Product of a Welsh public school and articled to a firm of well-known Pontowyn solicitors, a non-smoking social drinker, Lewis had for fifteen years been a good family man. As a youngster he had been a "bit wild with the girls," according to his late father, but at the age of twenty-one had married Ann, a beautiful, dark-haired local girl, which made him the envy of every young male in Pontowyn. Ann's widowed mother was anxious for the match, Lewis' parents not enthusiastic. Their son had yet to qualify, and they felt Ann to be a class beneath them. He could have married better, if less attractive, girls. Siân, their only child, was born a year later. After Siân had gone to school, Ann had continued working for the Social Services department of the local authority. Lewis had worked for the Pontowyn solicitors after qualifying, and at the age of twenty-six had received a partnership. The firm had continued to do well. Lewis was the senior partner but one.

Sir Nigel Appleton had contacted him a week previously. Appleton represented a multi-national corporation negotiating a land purchase near Pontowyn. Appleton wanted a local man to deal with the vendors' solicitors, to be on the spot and take instructions from Stansgate Appleton. The corporation, Aberinvest, had wide and diverse interests, some in West Wales. Appleton was obviously trying out Lewis' firm. The potential business would be inexhaustible. Lewis was both excited and nervous.

Appleton approached Lewis. They had never met, but the maître d'hôtel pointed Lewis out. Lewis had no difficulty recognizing what was probably the best-known face in legal circles. As they entered the dining room, Lewis recognized one or two famous financial faces. Appleton nodded in several directions, acknowledging half the diners. At least it seemed that way to Lewis.

"You'll take another sherry," Appleton invited as they perused the menu. "And I should try the Beluga, frightfully good. I always enjoy spending Aberinvest's money. Goodness knows they have enough of it, even in these strictured times. Their chairman spends a great deal of time down in your neck of the woods. Bit of a recluse these days by all accounts. Has very little to do with the company now. Young fellow like yourself—name of Wyatt. I'm told he's interested in this particular agricultural purchase. Ever run across him?"

"Can't say I have," Lewis replied. "But if I were spending two million pounds, I'm sure I'd take an interest."

"Money doesn't interest him. Then only the extremely affluent can afford that luxury. On the very rare occasions they want him, he's always fishing. Do you fish?"

"Occasionally. I'm not the world's greatest."

"Wyatt owns the best stretches in West Wales. I'll mention it to Fallon, Aberinvest's managing director."

"That's very kind of you, Sir Nigel."

They discussed the legal position of Aberinvest's agricultural purchases. Over coffee and cognac, Lewis showed Appleton the deeds and contracts signed by the vendors. Appleton was pleased with the acquisition of a competent local man. Just before they parted, he withdrew his notepad from the briefcase, tore off two pieces of paper and handed them to Lewis.

Outside Romulus the eight-man tail split into two sections. The first followed Appleton, the second Lewis. Richard Lansbury reported the meeting to Quittenden by radio. Calladyne and Vicky Keane were dispatched on Q's direct orders to take over the surveillance of Lewis. By the time they had made contact, Lewis had been down Oxford Street, through Harrods and several other shops. Eventually he took a taxi to Paddington Station, where he boarded the 4:05 Inter-City for West Wales. He had spoken to no one except shop assistants and the taxi driver.

Calladyne and Vicky Keane had been instructed to follow Lewis wherever he went. Vicky Keane managed to call in before the train left Paddington and her radio transmitter was out of Quittenden's range.

They both sat in the first-class carriage in seats across the gangway from Lewis. He spent the journey working on papers from his briefcase, and when he went to the refreshment coach, took the briefcase with him. Calladyne followed, expecting some action. The disappointment of none was mollified by two large whiskies. Working for Q meant better expenses.

He looked out of the window as the train sped across the dunes and through the grey cloud that hung over Port Talbot. At Swansea, where the train stopped for fifteen minutes, he called in to S.I.S. operations room, which took a message for Quittenden and gave him one in return. A backup unit had reached the M4 at Cardiff and was heading westward. They would wait in a Swansea hotel for Calladyne's next call. The man they were following had to be identified.

At five past seven the train pulled into the county town of Pontowyn.

"Where the hell are we?" Calladyne enquired, as if expecting to see hostile tribesmen on the station platform.

"Nowhere I've heard of," Vicky Keane replied. "The man said follow him."

"Look friendly and pray for a taxi."

Pontowyn station had two small platforms and one old ticket collector who cheerfully accepted tickets from the handful of passengers. Vicky Keane felt the chill that always surrounds railway stations, and searched for the tickets she hoped had taken them as far as they had travelled. Calladyne shifted aggressively as the collector looked at the tickets and then at both of them.

"Llandewi is the next stop."

"Change of plans." Vicky Keane smiled.

The old man had not seen such an attractive girl that week.

"Nos da." He smiled, touching his cap.

Calladyne took her arm, and they walked on.

"What did he say?"

"Something in Welsh?" She shrugged her shoulders.

They watched David Lewis unlock a two-litre Cortina car and put his briefcase and bundle of packages into the back. Calladyne noted the registration number while Vicky Keane pointed out a single taxi some distance down the road.

"Call that number in. I'll follow him. You stay here till I make contact. Got your handset?"

"Yes, O master. Calladyne, why do I get all the best assignments?"

"You women want the equal opportunities."

He hailed the taxi and looked coldly at the driver, a long-haired, smiling, dark, young man.

"Police," Calladyne intoned.

The smile vanished. Calladyne got into the front of the taxi.

"I'm not inspecting licences or looking for bald tyres. Just drive where and when I say. Understand?"

The taxi driver looked at Calladyne's unsmiling face and general physical appearance, glancing briefly at the wallet Calladyne flipped open for a split second. He thought he'd seen some kind of badge. But he was not going to labour the point. This man would not want to answer any questions.

"Off you go, that way." Calladyne pointed in the direction David Lewis' Cortina had taken.

The taxi was an ageing Austin Maxi, but the engine was obviously kept in good order. Calladyne lit a cigarette, his trained eyes observing the ground they covered. Traffic was light as they drove into the town along what appeared to be the main street. The driver responded to Calladyne's instructions silently and quickly, halting some twenty yards past David Lewis' parked Cortina. The narrow street appeared to be the town's financial and legal quarter.

Calladyne noticed a phone box on the opposite side of the deserted street.

"Wait here till I come back, chum," he ordered.

Once in the phone box he picked up the receiver as a cover. Using his hand transmitter he contacted Vicky Keane.

"Vehicle registered to David Lewis, Pen y banc, Llan something or other."

"Spell it," Calladyne ordered. "Right now he's used a key to gain entry to solicitor's offices in Teilo Street. Pritchard, Roberts, Evans & Son. What does Q say?"

"Don't use local cops. Keep a low profile but keep watching."

"Enigmatic."

"Calladyne, my little profile is getting cold here. There are plumbers on the way. Q wants surveillance and maybe entry. He wants those papers Appleton gave Lewis."

Calladyne watched Lewis emerge from the offices without his briefcase.

"Briefcase is in the office. I'll tail him. You go and find us a hotel."

"I will do," Vicky Keane replied. "Separate rooms. I don't have my overnight bag."

"I always sleep very light." Calladyne leered. "See you."

The taxi driver was still in position. Calladyne slammed the door shut.

"Follow that car is it?" the driver asked.

"Got it in one, boyo."

They drove out of Pontowyn on the main West Wales road for two miles before turning right onto a country lane. Calladyne observed cattle, hills, sheep, and cornfields in a landscape of scattered farms and descending sun. They met no traffic except an old Mini and a tractor. Four miles further on they were in the village of Llandewi where Calladyne noticed a post office, two pubs, a shop, and a cluster of houses. Half a mile beyond the village David Lewis' Cortina turned left into a driveway. A detached square house stood back thirty yards from the road in half an acre of garden. The garage doors were open. Parked inside was a white MGB sports car. Lewis drove the Cortina alongside, got out and closed the garage door. He walked to the front door of the house where he used his own key.

"Shit," Calladyne exclaimed.

"Sorry." The driver turned to him.

"Never mind. How much?"

"You getting out here?—Sorry, five pounds forty."

Calladyne gave the driver seven pounds.

"Keep your mouth shut," he warned.

The driver did not need telling twice. He pocketed the money and drove off, relieved to be rid of his unpleasant fare.

Calladyne waited until the car had driven out of sight, then used his handset again. The range was extreme but he contacted Vicky Keane.

"Is that backup unit here from Swansea yet?"

"Just arrived."

"Send them out here. Have they brought us a spare car?"

"Indeed."

"Come with 'em and pick me up."

*****

David Lewis was welcomed home by Skipper, the mongrel dog, a cat, his daughter Siân, and finally his wife Ann, who emerged from the kitchen. He kissed wife and daughter, patted the dog, and almost fell over the cat.

"Home comes the hunter bearing gifts. Close your eyes, everyone. Skipper, out of the way."

Lewis handed presents to both Siân and Ann. While they opened them he took a cold beer from the fridge and went through to an open-plan lounge dining room. He stood looking out of the window, across the fields to the setting sun. He was pleased with himself. Sir Nigel Appleton had been impressed with his work.

Shrieks of delight could be heard from the kitchen as first Siân, then his wife threw their arms around him. He had bought his daughter an expensive perfume gift set. For his wife, a silk kimono.

"By way of celebration," he explained.

Lewis put his arms around his wife, partly in guilt for having bought his secretary a pearl necklace and partly for self-assurance. Ann Lewis was a beautiful woman. She stood just over five feet six. Her black evening dress, cut low, revealed elegant shoulders and a cleavage that still interested him. The close-cropped black hair accentuated her fine classical good looks. The dark brown eyes gazed into his as she whispered.

"Good day?"

He could see the dining table set with candles and a bottle of wine.

"Yes," he replied. "Where's Siân gone?"

"Mair Edwards is collecting her in ten minutes. She's staying with Alison tonight and tomorrow. They're having a party—supervised of course."

"Which leaves us—alone." Lewis smiled.

Ann sat him on the sofa.

"Tell me then."

"Sir Nigel Appleton gave me a very expensive lunch. He was very impressed by my negotiating powers and the standard of legal work."

"Go on, you." Ann Lewis laughed.

"True. Anyway, Aberinvest is a multi-national—varied interests—quite a few in West Wales. And I've been promised most if not all their legal work down here. Who's a clever boy, then?"

"David, that's fabulous. Drink?"

"I'm fine with the beer."

Ann Lewis poured herself a gin and tonic.

"I called in at the office on the way home. There was a message on the answering machine from Aberinvest's managing director, no less. He thinks their chairman is in Dysant, and could I take these documents up personally tomorrow morning. He lives there, by all accounts. Have you run across him, man named Wyatt?"

"No. Why should I?"

"Thought you might have—with the council work." Lewis shrugged.

"I don't think Social Services would be needed by the chairman of a multi-national, do you?—Now you haven't forgotten we're going to look at that pony for Siân, have you? I've got the afternoon off."

"I won't be long. If I leave the office at nine-thirty I'll be back here by twelve-thirty. Better still, I'll meet you in that little hotel by the river in Dysant at twelve. They do a good lunch."

Chapter Six

Quittenden's plumbers went in at 0105 on Wednesday, August 25. They were a crack team who could spike a high-security building in under an hour. The solicitor's offices in Pontowyn were protected by a single burglar alarm, which took the two electronics men twenty-four seconds to isolate. The cracksman was through the front door in three seconds and inside David Lewis' office in thirty. He copied the documents contained in the briefcase and the relevant page of the desk diary. One electronics man planted microphones throughout the office and in the telephone system, the second recorded messages on the answering machine. By 0130 the plumbers were away from their target location and by 0230 were telephoning the information into Quittenden's computer from a safe house thirty miles away.

While this was going on, Calladyne was sitting in the woods not two hundred yards from David Lewis' house. The bedroom light had gone off at twelve-fifteen and Calladyne was wishing he and David Lewis could change places. That wife of his was something. He thought of Vicky Keane, sleeping in a local hotel, and cursed his luck for not being there. She probably wouldn't have him. It was against the rules, but a man can always try.

The plumbers' information had been evaluated by Quittenden, sitting alone at his computer terminal by 0305. He began to smell blood. A telephone call to a sleepy porter in a Pontowyn hotel roused Vicky Keane from sleep at 0330 and she was ordered to be back in London with Calladyne by 1100. Then he lit a cigarette, poured himself some black coffee, and started making telephone calls from one of his two direct lines.

He was surprised by a visit from Llewellyn Jones at just after 0405. The portly Welshman had been roused by the Prime Minister on a domestic political matter because the House was having one of its periodic all-night sittings.

"So I thought I'd pop around." Llewellyn Jones smiled. He accepted the coffee from Quittenden and sat himself in the armchair.

"Been to bed, Q?"

Quittenden indicated the camp bed.

"Catnapping. I'm onto something. Interested?"

"Certainly am."

Facsimiles of the various information flashed on the screen. First was a message in Appleton's writing on a piece of paper torn from a notepad.

RE. CONTRACT. FALLON TO CALL THIS EVENING. WILL AD-
VISE LOCATION WYATT. ROUTES A AND B UNACCEPTABLE. WY-
ATT IN AGREEMENT.

Then the tape recording of the message from Peter Fallon of
Aberinvest was played. Notes in David Lewis' desk diary and
cancelled appointments for Wednesday, August 25, flashed onto
the screen. Then there was an address and directions to it, under
the name of Wyatt.

There followed a recording of Sir Nigel Appleton's telephone
call to Aberinvest's offices in London.

"This is from surveillance on Appleton," Quittenden indicated.

Llewellyn Jones nodded.

"Fallon," the recording began with a man answering his telephone. Then Appleton's voice. "Peter. Nigel Appleton here.
I've seen my man. All is in order. Now we need Wyatt."

"I'll call Lewis' offices later today with a location. Give me
the number. Pontowyn four-three-seven-five, got it. Thank you
Nigel."

Llewellyn Jones lit a cigar and puffed thoughtfully.

"Any more?"

"A ten-page contract," Quittenden replied, pressing a switch
on the console. He had all ten pages in view simultaneously on
five screens.

"What a clever toy," Llewellyn Jones remarked. "No mention of routes in this contract? No. I see." Llewellyn Jones
sipped his coffee and thought for a moment.

"Any known connection between Fallon, Lewis, Wyatt, and
Moresby?"

Quittenden flicked more buttons, like a small child playing
with a new present.

"Connection Wyatt and Sir Philip Moresby." The screen
flashed again. "1. Source—interrogation Dorothy Burton.
S.S.D. Personnel File No. 3482/D/4. 22.8.81 Quotation. As far
as I know he has spent every Christmas for the last four years at
least with a Mr. Wyatt, down in West Wales. 2. Source—S.S.D.

File No. 110/A/3/70. Operations code Gamma Red. Clearance please?''

Llewellyn Jones looked at the screen in amazement.

"What's happening, Q?''

"This computer is linked to all the available information sources I require. You saw me ask it for any connection between Moresby and our three names. The first connection shows up on Mrs. Burton's interview on Monday when she was asked if she knew any of Moresby's friends, where he went on holiday. Computer located that: no problem. But it's asked me for my security clearance because we've gone on to an S.S.D. file number that denotes an agent or past agent involved in Gamma Red operations. There's source information here which won't be released until I put in my security clearance code.''

"Put mine in,'' Llewellyn Jones invited, handing his green pass to Quittenden, who smiled to himself.

The computer screen flickered.

"Insufficient clearance. Repeat Operation Code Gamma Red.''

Llewellyn Jones looked uncomfortable.

"What's the damn thing up to?''

"Your security clearance is insufficient for the computer to divulge details of a Gamma Red operation,'' Quittenden replied. "The computer has noted that you're political rather than Intelligence personnel.''

"How very astute of it. Meaning?''

"Gamma Red operations are those of considerable political sensitivity. I'll use my clearance.''

Within seconds the computer replied.

"2. Source S.S.D. File No. 110/A/3/70. Gamma Red Operation Alpha Delta 342/X. Wyatt, Major secondment S.A.S. to S.S.D. on request head S.S.D. Operation objective. Release Prince Feizal Saud held by Black September. Operation control Head S.S.D. Operation complete success.''

Quittenden then typed in the S.S.D. file number shown. The computer replied again.

"Wyatt. Born 1947. Education unspecified. Sandhurst 1964. Commissioned South Wales Borderers 1965. Transferred Special Air Service 1966. May 1967, secret secondment Israeli Defence Forces. Action. Six Day War 25th Independent Parachute Regiment. Assault on Scopus. Decorated. Transferred anti-Fedayeen ops West Bank 1968. Secondment to Sultanate of Oman. Captain. Personal bodyguard Sheikh Abdullah Baquoos. Decorated 1969 saving life of Abdullah Baquoos. July 1970 transferred to S.S.D. on request Head S.S.D. Success Prince Feizal Saud release. Decorated. 1971 resigned commission and S.S.D."

Llewellyn Jones said, "Very informative. Is this the same Wyatt who is chairman of Aberinvest?"

"Let's see," Quittenden replied. The computer responded.

"July 1971. Began business import export Middle East. Contacts in both Israel, Gulf, Arab States. Jan 1972. Bought control Aberinvest. 1981 January. Resigns Managing Director Aberinvest Ltd. Maintains seat on board non-executive chairman. Voting shares held 58%. Non-voting shares held 52%."

Llewellyn Jones poured himself more coffee. Quittenden relaxed into his desk chair.

"Surely a man in that position can't be Moresby's escape route, Q?"

"Aberinvest is the second-biggest multi-national in Europe. They have wealth, influence, power. Their ex-chairman was an army of one fifteen years ago. Knowing what you do about certain conglomerates L.J., would you be surprised if this Wyatt considers himself above the law?"

"He's hardly likely to be working for Moscow Centre, though, is he? I mean he could buy it."

Quittenden smiled.

"There is such a thing as loyalty and friendship. To spend Christmas with a man, you either have to be a good friend or very lonely."

"Yes, one doesn't think of friendship and loyalty as a motive these days. Tends to have gone out of fashion."

"In your line of country as well, L.J."

"Q, I do believe that somewhere you have a sense of humour. That was almost a joke."

Quittenden rose from his chair, ignoring Llewellyn Jones' remark.

"So we'll see where Mr. Wyatt leads us."

"I hope that any action needed will be speedily undertaken. I'm beginning to worry about this Moresby business, Q. The sooner he is put in the dock or out of the way, the better I will feel. Then perhaps we can all return to some sanity."

"Surely that is a Prime Ministerial decision," Quittenden replied.

Llewellyn Jones opened the door.

"From what I've seen of you, Q, the decision will be yours. Any higher authority will merely be a rubber stamp."

Quittenden closed the door behind him. He smiled. He had smelt blood.

The telephone wakened Nury al Said at 5:05 A.M. He was hazy after too much alcohol and very tired. Trying to slide across his bed to reach the ringing intrusion, he encountered a sleeping obstacle. He turned on the light, blinked at the mop of blond hair, and threw back the sheet to reveal a naked female of elegant proportions. He now knew why he felt so tired and tried to remember her name, but all European women had strange names. The telephone rang insistently. He groped for the receiver and grunted.

"You know the time?"

"Listen. Your Irish associate will be with you in ten minutes. Your objective and down payment has just been put through your letter box. The transaction must be effected immediately."

"Eh."

"Immediately." The line went dead with a single click. But Said had exact recall of the words.

Leaning over, he slapped a white female buttock hard.

"Get up. You're leaving."

The blond sat bolt upright, revealing a large pair of breasts and a face smeared with mascara. She rubbed her eyes.

"What—?"

"You're leaving, you stupid bitch. Now."

"Christ, it's only five o'clock." The voice was pure Chelsea: "Look, you unpleasant tent-dwelling nomad, I'll leave when I'm good and ready."

She flopped back on the bed. Nury's strong right hand seized her shoulder, turning her over. His left hand went to her right breast, fingers seizing the nipple and squeezing.

"You bastard!" the girl screamed, and struggled. Nury laughed and pressed down on her with his body. Pain tore through her. She kept screaming until she had no breath left to scream.

Nury released his grip.

"Now get out."

The girl fought for breath, blue eyes wide with fear. She scrambled for the clothes scattered on the floor. Nury had gone downstairs and picked up a bulky envelope. As the girl ran past him on the stairs, pulling a dress over her head, he opened the front door for her, kicked her, and laughed.

In five minutes Nury had examined the envelope and checked its contents. Inside was a photograph, on the back of which two names and an address were written. The remainder of the envelope was filled with money. A quick count told Nury twenty percent of the contract price of £10,000 had been paid.

Within ten minutes Nury had cleared the flat of his one suit of clothes, toothbrush, and towel. He had clipped a nine-mm Makarov automatic pistol into a shoulder holster. As he left the flat a 2.3-litre blue Cortina drew up. Nury got in the passenger seat.

This hit would be quick, clean, and easily paid. Nury had dealt with this anonymous client before.

Bannion was driving. He had hired the car with a fictitious driving licence the day before and paid in cash. He always drove a hired car, and always had one available. Only amateurs stole vehicles for a job.

They drove westward from London on the M4, joining the five-thirty juggernauts and rigidly observing the speed limit. Even Mad Jack Bannion would not invite trouble from motorway cruise cars when on the job. He had learned to drive as a fourteen-year-old in the streets of Belfast in stolen cars. His expertise brought him to the notice of a certain organization that specialized in shooting up Protestant areas. Graduating to chauffeur the front-line assassination squads, he proved he could drive a getaway vehicle over, under, or around anything. Taking his turn with the gun, he murdered two part-time U.D.R. soldiers as they quietly went about their civilian business. He was adept at beating old men and women whom the district committee decided to discipline and proficient at kneecapping recalcitrant traders refusing to pay protection money. In any other European city Bannion would have been classed as a vicious, murderous young thug. In Belfast he was a soldier of the Provisional I.R.A.

Three incidents had determined Mad Jack Bannion too dangerous, a liability through wanton violence, even to his Republican associates. He had kicked to death a pregnant woman whose only crime had been to offer comfort to a dying British squaddie. Even in the Falls Road area, this was going too far. Compounding his folly, Bannion casually murdered a local shopkeeper who had once refused him work as a newspaper delivery boy. But the final act in his career as a terrorist had been in South Armagh. Driving for a murder squad, ambushed by the S.A.S., Bannion departed at high speed when his first comrade was hit. He didn't stop driving until he reached Dublin. Catching the first ferry to the mainland, Bannion was in London when he heard his former comrades were looking for him. He never returned to the Emerald Isle. Instead, he made his way with the gun, as a contract assassin or wheelman—usually with Nury. The occupation became an obsession. Because Mad Jack Bannion liked killing people.

Nury al Said was the Lebanese son of middle-class parents. Rejecting their values but not their financial support, he had drifted into Fedayeen operations as an idealist revolutionary. A willing student of urban terror, he planted bombs in soft civilian targets. The leaders of Black June recognized potential and sent him to Libya, where Said came under the influence of disaffected

C.I.A. men training Quaddafi's soldiers of world revolution. He came to London at twenty-four as a student and full-fledged terrorist. After one minor operation he decided English girls, casinos, and night clubs were more his taste than the austere life-style of a Muslim crusader. To support his standard of living, he took to contract killing. To him it was a profession. He would have been equally content as a doctor or a lawyer, like his father.

Bannion and Nury al Said spoke little to each other. They had little in common except their purpose. Breakfast was taken at a motorway service station. By 10:30 A.M. they were studying an ordnance survey map of the Pontowyn area. Bannion likened the West Wales countryside to the Irish Border country. Said ventured no opinion. He located the address on the back of the photograph, indicating on the map to Bannion the best area to leave the Cortina for a fast getaway. Bannion nodded agreement.

"We look at it once, Bannion. Then we do the job."

A strange look came into Bannion's eyes. He smiled at Said, then looked down at the photograph. Suddenly, his right hand flashed over the photograph twice. Said saw the glint of metal.

The photograph was cut twice diagonally.

Chapter Seven

Ann Lewis was at her desk in the County offices by eight twenty-five on Wednesday, August 25. She had left her husband breakfasting, wearing the suit he had worn to London. Which made her think. Had he really been in London with Sir Nigel Appleton negotiating for business? It sounded too good to be true. The way David had described everything the future looked very financially secure. He had talked ambitiously of expanding the practice, even of branching out. And David was not an ambitious man.

Over the past few months he had also seemed to take more of a pride in his appearance. Never an untidy man, she thought, but he'd taken to using more after-shave than usual, and to cleaning his own shoes. On several occasions he had been home from the office later than usual, and muttered something about more work when casually asked. He would often sit watching television when she knew his mind was elsewhere. He had taken on a new secretary some months earlier—Rosalind something. Ann Lewis had met her, an attractive girl in an obvious way, early twenties. There had been a hint of jealousy in the girl's manner, an undercurrent of antagonism.

"I wonder what he brought her back from London," she asked herself.

She had always worked. It preserved her independence, and helping people in a practical, professional way interested her. Since her marriage, David had been the only man in her life. She had received numerous offers, and still did. At last year's office party, her boss had tried to guide her into a locked office. She had resisted with a severe verbal warning which went unheeded, followed by her knee being brought up sharply into the parts the alcohol had reached too quickly. When acquaintances confessed their aspirations or extramarital activities, she did sometimes think she was missing out, but the thoughts were fleeting. She still loved David.

By ten she had cleared her desk of the morning post. She could not stop thinking about David and his behaviour. The more she thought, the more she was prepared to read into it.

On an impulse she telephoned his office to find he was out. She asked to speak to Roz.

"I'm afraid she's out as well," the telephonist replied, somewhat reluctantly, Ann Lewis thought. David Lewis, you wouldn't be, would you? Not during working hours, she thought.

"Do you know where David is, by any chance? It's important I speak to him."

"He's gone to Dysant to see a client. There's no telephone I'm afraid. If you wait, I'll look in his diary for the address."

She felt slightly foolish waiting. David wouldn't take his secretary to see a client, would he?

"Mrs. Lewis, the address is Bwythyn-y-Wen, Dysant. Half a mile past the hotel on the Lampeter road, turning to the left. It's a private road. The address is marked on the roadside at the turning."

Ann Lewis put the telephone down. She went into her boss' office. He always helped her out when he could, hoping that one day he would be rewarded. She had finished her morning's work. She had already arranged for the afternoon off. He was quite content to let her leave early.

She glanced at her watch as she slowed the MGB down at Dysant bridge and looked into the hotel car park. She was due to meet David there at twelve-fifteen. It was now ten thirty-eight. She thought about waiting.

"Go on, Ann girl. If he is knocking his secretary off, you might as well know about it."

So she found the turning on the left, a narrow tarmac track between hedgerows. After a drive of half a mile, she found herself descending into a valley, wooded slopes rising on either side of the track that wound sharply to the left and emerged to a spectacular view. The land fell away to the right, revealing the sweep of the valley and meadows running down to some trees along a river. On the left, nestling at the foot of a wooded slope, broken by a tarmac circle, stood a two-storey, white-walled cottage. Her husband's car was parked on the tarmac next to an old well that had been restored, repointed, and the woodwork painted black.

There was no other vehicle in sight. The cottage was obviously inhabited, the paintwork recent and the lawn cut. She parked the MGB next to her husband's car and stood for some minutes looking at the scenery. The valley was so quiet. Sun shining through the trees cast shafts of light through the clearing. The river sounds whispered up the meadow. The view across the valley and beyond was breathtaking.

Feeling apprehensive about looking foolish if her husband really was with a client, she knocked on the cottage door and received no reply. She called and there was no answer. She turned the door handle and looked inside, inquisitively. She was in one vast room against the far wall of which was an open staircase. The walls were of rough stone. On the left of the room was a large stone fireplace above which hung a shotgun. Walls were decorated with genuine horse brasses mounted on black leather. In one corner of the room was a desk, and against the right-hand wall stood a real Welsh dresser, the shelves filled with books. The carpet was dark green, expensively practical. Two leather armchairs flanked the fireplace, where the large grate was made up but unlit.

But Ann Lewis' attention was rivetted on the leather settee, where a woman's brassière lay next to a silk dressing gown. On a small coffee table stood two empty bottles of wine and two glasses. A cut-glass ashtray contained three cigarette ends, which she examined. They all bore traces of lipstick.

"David Lewis," she shouted on impulse, starting involuntarily in anticipation of an answer from upstairs. There was none. She looked again at the brassière and again at the dressing gown. As she moved toward a door at the end of the room a voice almost whispered from behind her.

"Good morning."

She turned, startled, her hand automatically going to her chest. She had heard no one come in. She stood looking at a man slightly taller than she, slimly built but not skinny, age, she thought, about thirty-five. His face was almost gaunt, but quite good-looking, she decided, and had character. A smile played on his lips, and his eyes were almost black, matching the hair that curled to the collar of a fishing jacket. He took off a hat covered with flies and put a fishing rod in the corner of the room.

"You startled me," she replied, then after pausing for breath, "Am I in your house?"

"Yes." He smiled again.

"I'm very sorry," she apologized, confused by the appearance of this quiet man.

46

"Would you like a drink?" he offered. The voice was firm, educated. He sounded English. "You look as though you could do with one. Do it down. Sorry about the mess. My secretary hasn't tidied up after her—too much to drink." He looked at both glasses.

"Me too, I think." He picked up the dressing gown and brassière and put them at the foot of the stairs.

"Hope scotch is all right," he continued. "She finished off the gin as well."

The man withdrew an empty bottle from the Welsh dresser and put it on top. Taking a bottle of malt whisky, he poured two generous measures into glasses, handing Ann Lewis one as she sat on the settee, embarrassed, and not knowing what to say.

"I'm sorry for coming in," she apologized. "I'm looking for David Lewis, my husband. His car's outside."

"I'm expecting him. I didn't hear his car because I was fishing the Falls pool. On my way back I heard your car arrive. I watched you admiring the scenery. Thought you might be an early Christmas present. Disappointingly, you're married to the lucky Mr. Lewis."

"I didn't see anyone." Ann Lewis accepted a cigarette the man offered from a gold box on the mantelpiece. He lit it with a matching gold table lighter.

"You wouldn't have." He smiled again, sat himself in the armchair. "I didn't want you to."

She looked straight into his eyes. There was a presence about this man that fascinated her. As he spoke the last words she felt a chill go down her spine that vanished only when he smiled.

"I did leave a note telling your husband where I was. Perhaps he's gone for a stroll up the bank or—"

He broke off in mid-sentence as a sharp crack sounded. She thought he muttered to himself "nine mil." There were two more cracks. He was out of the chair like a cat, swiftly across to the desk drawer.

"Poachers again," he winked at her and reached up for the shotgun above the mantelpiece. "You stay here and if your husband comes in tell him I won't be long."

Then he vanished through the door.

Ann Lewis swallowed the rest of her drink. Her husband occasionally went shooting, and on several occasions she had accompanied him. His shotgun always sounded loud and booming. It didn't sound like the sharp cracks the man had said were poachers.

It was her day for acting on impulses, she thought, so let's go and have a look. She went out through the door near the stairs, found herself in a compact and very modern kitchen, and walked through an outside door onto a lawn bordered a hundred yards away by a line of fir trees. She was curious to see how this man dealt with poachers. She walked up the grassy slope and, as she emerged through the line of trees, she saw David.

He was staggering. The new suit was torn and dirty, his face scratched and bleeding. The shirt front was bloodsoaked. He stood upright for a moment, then fell face down, blood gushing from his mouth, a gurgling sound coming from deep in his throat.

She froze for a moment. Then she fell beside him, screaming, trying vainly to turn him, to see his face, to hold him, to help him. But she was seized from behind and thrown violently on her back to the ground. Scenes flashed before her in a series of unreal images. A man stood over her, holding a gun, his young face twisted into a grotesque smile as he roughly hauled her to her feet.

"Look what I've got, Nury." The voice was cold, chilling.

She could hear running footsteps behind him. He threw her to the ground again and stepped back.

"Now I'm going to kill you, darlin'." He laughed, stepping back again.

His finger curled around the pistol's trigger. Ann Lewis lay mesmerized by the sight of the gun, knowing she would die, powerless to save herself. A loud explosion sounded. The man was blown aside like a rag doll. Later, she thought she could recall an echo of the first boom while the man was still in midair because he jerked and was smashed flat to the ground.

She also thought she saw another man turn and fire into the

trees. He seemed to throw his gun away, run toward her, and look down at her for a second. She lay shocked into immobility, gazing at the man's black hair, darkly tanned skin, and thin moustache. Then he was gone.

Suddenly, a flash of mottled colouring landed across her, knocking the breath from her body. She realized the heavy weight was a man, breathing hard. A hot hand covered her mouth and a voice whispered in her ear.

"Lie still, Mrs. Lewis. Quiet. We've got to stay alive."

He moved her with his body, into the base of the trees, all the time covering her. At the same time his hands were reloading the shotgun, then groped for something on the grass beside her. She heard her car engine revving and tyres screaming. The man moved off her, both hands holding the pistol that had almost killed her.

"Christ," she heard him swear. Then he turned to her, protecting her again with his body.

"Stay still, Mrs. Lewis." The voice was calm and commanding.

As the car engine died away, the man moved quickly, his left hand touching the vein of David Lewis' neck. He didn't look at the other man.

She was on her feet now, struggling to reach her David. But the man held her away.

"He's dead."

She fought him, fingers clawing at his eyes, knee driving toward his groin. All her strength surged at him, she had to reach David. The man was too strong. She kept screaming and fighting. Then a series of stinging slaps hit her face. She stopped struggling and stared at the man whose grip held her wrists to her side. Shock had become hysteria, but the slaps brought her momentarily back to reality.

"He's dead. You'll do no good here. Let's move." The voice was cold, hard, angry. Even in her shocked state, it scared her.

The man half-carried her to the cottage, laid her on the settee. She only remembered part of what happened. Whisky was poured down her. She was given a cigarette. Images of David bleeding, the man with the gun, the second man, kept flashing before her eyes. She remembered the taste of whisky, drawing deeply on the cigarette. She was isolated, alone, devastated, and blindly terrified. Unable to control her hands she dropped the cigarette. Her head swirled, she was carried, retching, into another room.

She remembered cars, voices, policemen. A needle was thrust into her arm. Her head swirled again. The next thing she remembered was waking up on her bed at home.

The comfortable smile of Megan Roberts came into view as Ann Lewis looked around the bedroom. Siân was by the bedside, crying. Dr. Jack Harries' enormous hand felt her pulse.

"David," she sobbed. "David."

Then Megan Roberts was alone with her. Calm, capable, motherly Megan. Pillar of the W.I., W.R.V.S. and wife of Arthur Roberts, David's senior partner.

"Steady now girl, you've had a terrible time," she comforted.

"Does Siân know?"

"And being very brave about it. We'll stay with you. Now try and get some sleep. Dr. Jack has left you some tablets."

Ann Lewis swallowed two of the tablets while Megan held the glass. The images receded as Ann Lewis drifted into sleep.

Chapter Eight

Nury al Said was now a man terrified by his own shadow. He had seen Bannion shoot at David Lewis and hit him in the shoulder. Lewis had fallen, but then rose and ran toward the house. Bannion had given chase and shot again, hitting Lewis in the back. Either that mad Irishman was trying to kill the target slowly or his first aim had been bad. But the target kept on running. Dead on his feet, he must have been, and he still kept going.

Then he saw Bannion had reached Lewis, and was throwing a girl around. She must have come from the house, he thought. A good-looking girl, but no time to fool around with her. Bannion, get it over with. Then a stunning blast, a rolling echo as Bannion was hurled to tattered oblivion. Nury spotted movement in bushes to his right. He aimed the Makarov instinctively, firing fast. His target was a blur, flashing across spaces thirty yards away. On his fourth shot, the Makarov jammed. But he had lost his target. He looked down at the girl. She had seen him, could identify him. Bannion's killer was moving, trying to reach the girl.

Nury had had enough. Weaponless, he ran through the fir trees and saw the cars. The white MGB, its top down, had the keys in the ignition. He drove off, burning rubber as the car veered and swung along the narrow tarmac track. Two hundred yards away, he almost forced an old van off the main road and pulled alongside the Cortina. He threw the MGB keys over a hedge and revved the Cortina hard. At last he was away.

He needed traffic. There would be police cars about soon, probably from the direction of Pontowyn. Within ten minutes he was lost in the tourist traffic on the main Lampeter road. Making a right turn, he headed in the direction of Brecon. Driving within the speed limit he made for a motorway. Now he needed the anonymity of the city. His getaway car had not been spotted, he was almost certain.

The target was dead, and so was Bannion. There were two witnesses to the killing. The girl would be no problem to dispose of. The man—the man was a professional. He had killed Bannion instantly with a shotgun at thirty yards, and managed to keep the spread away from the girl. He had run toward her, weaving, using cover like a man who was used to combat—real combat.

Nury made a quick decision. His principal in the contract would not be happy with the loose ends. But the £2,000 down payment was in Nury's pocket. England was no longer for him. He abandoned the Cortina in a side street off the Cromwell Road, made a telephone call from a public box. A voice he knew answered.

Nury al Said went to ground.

Detective Chief Superintendent Dan Caswell lit a Capstan Full Strength and coughed loudly. The dark-haired Woman Detective Sergeant with him smiled and ventured an opinion.

"I thought you'd given up, sir."

"Until yesterday I had," he grumbled, walking to the window of Ann Lewis' lounge and looking across the field. Involuntarily he checked his watch. 9:30 A.M., Thursday, August 26, and he had not slept. The killing of David Lewis had upset him, the manner of it had angered him, its results worried him. He could not forget the haunted face of the fourteen-year-old girl he had met in the hallway. Megan Roberts had taken her off to another part of the house. He was not looking forward to interviewing the widow. He was thankful for the presence of Arthur Roberts, an old friend and Lewis' partner.

"My twenty-seventh murder," Caswell confided to the W.D.S. "And I can't get used to the survivors' grief."

"We'll have him, sir," the W.D.S. confidently replied.

"It's not the second man I'm worried about. They were professionals. It's the bastard behind it I'm after," he said quietly.

She studied him. At forty-six he had been head of C.I.D. for the largest police area in Britain for five years. He was a wiry man, dark-haired, with pale blue eyes that bored into a suspect's soul. Sometimes quick-tempered, he had a foxy smile, a cunning manner, and a reputation for having solved every murder he had ever investigated.

The lounge door opened and Caswell turned to see Arthur Roberts come through, supporting Ann Lewis on his arm. Caswell smiled sympathetically.

Rarely had he seen such an attractive woman. Attired in black, from shoes to the high-necked blouse, she moved gracefully. The mourning clothes could not take away the harrowed dignity in her high-cheekboned face, the beautiful sorrow in her liquid eyes. She sat in an armchair. Roberts offered her a cigarette, which Caswell lit for her.

"Mrs. Lewis, I can't express how sorry we all are. Your late husband was a fine, well respected man," Caswell sympathized, thinking to himself he sounded like a Methodist preacher and should start behaving like a policeman.

"Thank you," Ann Lewis replied.

"I know this isn't easy," he continued. "I've read your statement. Now are you sure that the first man stood over you and said 'Look what I've got, Nury'?"

"I won't forget those words or the look on his face, ever."

"I understand." Caswell moved on quickly. "And you'd recognize the second man, Nury, clearly?"

"I won't ever forget his face."

"I'd like you to look at some photographs which Detective Sergeant Jones will show you. If you can identify the man I'd like you to make a statement to that effect."

Ann Lewis nodded.

"Thank you." He turned to the door. Her voice stopped him.

"Mr. Caswell. Why David? What did he ever do to anyone?"

Caswell looked at her.

"I don't know why, Mrs. Lewis. If it's any consolation to you, I'll find out. Sooner or later I'll find out."

As he spoke the last words he was making himself a promise.

Arthur Roberts followed him out. They had known each other for years, respected each other's professional abilities.

"What do you think, Dan?"

"I need a motive. I know how Lewis was killed, who killed him. I've ruled her out as a suspect, and you, and virtually everyone else local. Lewis was working for this man Wyatt. I've spoken to his company and Sir Nigel Appleton. I've checked with the Met., and we're piecing together his time in London. I spent three hours with Wyatt yesterday. He gave me a full statement, off his own bat, no solicitor present. Damn shame those two weren't after him instead of poor Lewis."

"Why?"

"I've got a feeling they'd both be bloody dead and I wouldn't have to interview grieving victims. World's arse backwards. My chief wanted to prosecute Wyatt for killing that man. Still, one day we might start worrying about the victims instead of trying to mollycoddle the thugs."

"Wyatt sent a man here last night." Roberts looked puzzled. "A very tactful, highly intelligent public relations man. Didn't see Ann, of course. Told me that if anything was needed, doctors, hospitals, accommodation, funeral arrangements, anything at all, get it done very well and send him the bill. Guilty conscience, do you suppose?"

Caswell shook his head.

"No. Conscience perhaps. He's a strange fellow, chairman of Aberinvest the multi-national, semi-retired from what I gather. Hell of a boy a few years back. S.A.S. and all that nonsense. He said, 'Lewis was working for me, had come to my house and someone killed him. That's not on, Caswell,' he said, 'I feel responsible!' Then he said, 'They were pros, Caswell, make sure you protect your witness. Because if you don't, I will.' Then he went off in a helicopter to Cei Bach with three characters who looked like they'd make a mess of any two front rows in the world. Interesting fact being that the man he killed was a former I.R.A. thug called Bannion."

"Curious," Roberts replied.

"You can trust him, though, Arthur. I get that feeling. So don't be ungracious to him."

At the same time as Detective Chief Superintendent Dan Caswell left the Lewis house, a Sikorsky helicopter owned by Aberinvest landed at Ty Newydd, a country house near Cei Bach on the Cardigan coast. Its occupants were Peter Fallon, thirty-two-year-old managing director of Aberinvest, and Mrs. Dorothy Burton, Sir Philip Moresby's secretary.

On Monday, August 23, Dorothy Burton's world had collapsed around her. Sir Philip Moresby had been arrested for espionage. She had been interrogated by a slip of a red-headed girl with a Roedean accent who had refused to give her name. Then she had been driven to Whitehall to be interviewed by Llewellyn Jones.

She knew him through Sir Philip. Everything she disliked about the Welsh seemed to be personified by Llewellyn Jones. He lectured her in the manner of a non-conformist minister. He told her she was suspended from duty until further notice, that she was to have no contact with anyone from her work, and that she was to remain silent about Moresby's arrest. She was not to leave the country. He had ordered her passport confiscated and warned her that if she left London, she should advise Quittenden of S.I.S. before going.

She had spent from Monday night until Wednesday morning alone in her flat, eating little, sleeping fitfully, smoking endless cigarettes, and drinking a great deal of gin. She was normally a non-smoking teetotaller.

She could not forgive them for the treatment of Sir Philip Moresby, a man she had worked with and been more than a little in love with for twenty years. Yes, he was devious, cunning, unprincipled to those who knew him professionally. But she had seen the same man as S.I.S. Controller East Europe weep tears at the loss of two agents when he thought no one was looking. He had emerged from the operations room after seventy-two sleepless hours, mentally and physically exhausted, yet worked on, meeting, discussing, dealing, desperately seeking the solution that would bring his men out. She had seen him die a little each time the I.R.A. exploded a bomb in mainland Britain, killing and maiming civilians, and all the time beg for political permission to alert his agents to assassinate known I.R.A. leaders. She had once seen the row of medals awarded him for two years' hard, dangerous, mind-shattering work in France with the S.O.E., medals he never wore to the Cenotaph on Remembrance Day. Others deserved them far more, he would say.

Now he was branded a traitor. She feared for his safety. Were there no friends to fight for him? Would one member of the Security establishment lift a sherry glass to help him, even to wish him luck? She tried to rationalize her emotions. Moresby had always told her that emotional reactions were fatal in Intelligence work.

By Wednesday morning she had overcome her emotions. Either Moresby was innocent, or he was guilty. They were saying he was guilty. She had gathered a few facts from her interrogation. The picture was not favourable. Moresby had once said to her, "It is very easy in the Intelligence world to draw from the same basic facts two vastly different conclusions—one innocent, the other very sinister." Someone, somewhere, might draw innocent conclusions.

She pulled herself together and ate breakfast. In her address book were some numbers that Sir Philip Moresby often asked her to contact. She had memorized those numbers, as a good secretary would. One number he called perhaps twice a year. But always near Christmas time he would call. Then she would be asked to go out and collect a Christmas present that Moresby had ordered. Last year it had been an antique flintlock pistol. "For Wyatt," Moresby would say, and always follow with, "You know, Dorothy, I sometimes think you and he are the only real friends I have." She had once almost convinced herself he was talking in code.

So she left her flat and went for a walk. Although not a trained agent, she knew how to lose a tail. But no one followed her. So she used an inconspicuous public phone box and called the number.

Mr. Wyatt was unavailable, and no one knew where he was. The next man in seniority was Mr. Fallon, who was out all day. "Who was this calling?"

So she went to the library and looked up Aberinvest in a trade directory. By late afternoon she had worked out who Mr. Fallon was, his address and telephone number. There was no reply at his telephone number so she went round to his address in a fashionable and expensive Mayfair mews.

At eleven o'clock that night he arrived. She had some difficulty persuading him how important it was that she contact

Mr. Wyatt, especially since she would give no reason. Eventually Fallon decided to call Mr. Wyatt and tell him an attractive forty-year-old woman needed to see him personally, as a matter of urgency, but would not give her name.

It transpired that Mr. Wyatt was very anxious to see the anonymous lady. He had experienced a full, active, and very perplexing day, and would the lady mind accompanying Mr. Fallon on a helicopter flight very early in the morning. She refused to leave the flat now that she had made contact. Fallon decided she was not some kind of kook who forced her attention on young men, and let her have the bedroom while he spent the next four hours dozing fitfully on the sofa.

He slept better in the helicopter while the attractive blond woman chatted to the pilot about instruments, weather conditions, and radio communications. She woke him when they landed. He was curious to find out more.

Llewellyn Jones visited Quittenden again at nine-thirty on the morning of Thursday, August 26. Quittenden was playing with the computer again. A secretary brought coffee, and Llewellyn Jones placed a report on Quittenden's desk.

"I've read it, Q. Did you eliminate Lewis?"

"Don't be absurd. If I had, we wouldn't have policemen running about all over the place."

"What's your view? That report only states facts."

"Assume Lewis was Moresby's contact with Wyatt, the instrument of Moresby's personal independent escape route—nothing to do with Moscow Centre. Centre wants to exchange him. They want him back the safe, reliable way. So they arrange for Lewis to have an accident. Only they mistime and it comes out as murder. He was killed on Wyatt's ground before he got to Wyatt."

"How did they know about Lewis?"

"Somebody told them."

"Q. Only you and I knew about Lewis."

Quittenden lit a cigarette.

"Really, L.J. My agents knew about Lewis. So did Nigel Appleton. I don't think either of us or my agents are bent. I'm not sure about Appleton."

"He's under surveillance."

"I took it off after he met Lewis. You politicians are the cost-conscious ones. Surveillance was way over budget before this Moresby business started. I had the D.G. of Five on to me saying some Treasury chap was bitching this morning about overspending. Not that I take any notice."

"Was Lewis under surveillance when he met Wyatt?"

"Certainly not. I'd made arrangements to follow both parties later in the day. They were meeting in rural Wales, L.J. Their actual discussion wasn't important. The consequential action was."

"So you think that Moscow Centre arranged the killing?"

"Mad Jack Bannion was the deceased killer. My information is that he operated with Nury al Said, Lebanese playboy. We're looking for Said at the moment—actively. Hopefully we find him before Centre does."

"The police investigation continues."

Quittenden smiled.

"I was hoping you'd do something for me, L.J."

Llewellyn Jones wondered which computer he was dealing with.

"Continue." He was almost apprehensive about the next move.

"Have a word with the police down in the sticks. Put your Home Office hat on and ask them to leave it to us. Get that Caswell bloodhound off the scent of killers and back on to chasing sheep or something."

"What's Mr. Wyatt's next move?"

"That will be interesting. This is turning into a very complex little game. Moresby still steadfastly refuses to confess. Meanwhile let's see what Centre's next move is."

Chapter Nine

I knew the solicitor Lewis was coming that morning so I'd left a note pinned to the cottage door and walked down to the Falls pool. The fish weren't taking but there was a twenty-pound salmon lurking under bushes against the far bank. I wanted him out.

He knew more than I did. The sun was climbing higher, the water rushing, the fields green, the time going on. So I gave him best and walked back toward the cottage. I heard the car come down the driveway and stop. The pathway up goes through thick bushes and comes out looking down on the well and the turning area. On impulse I stopped and peeped round the old oak tree.

She wasn't my solicitor. I'd never seen her before. But she had style. She stood about five six, short black hair curling over the collar of a well-cut blazer. At a range of ten yards I could see high cheekbones, and the kind of beauty born of wild open spaces. She moved gracefully toward the cottage. I waited for a while and eventually she called out after receiving no reply. I waited for her to go in. She had to. She seemed that kind of a girl.

I got inside without her hearing me. I said good morning and she turned. The dark pools of eyes flashed. I just smiled and she looked embarrassed. I offered her a drink, then realized Sam had left half her underwear draped around the lounge. I explained briefly and could only find Glenmorangie. She sat down, apologizing for the intrusion, but had I seen her husband.

I knew she was married. The wide gold band on the third finger told me as much. Then she disappointed me by saying Lewis. When it comes to women I'm an old-fashioned pirate who knows enough to stay away from the wives of friends, colleagues, employees, and agents. Which was a shame, because her shape was classic under the blazer and tight trousers, and her perfume was expensive but discreet. I told her I hadn't seen her husband and perhaps he had gone for a walk. Then I heard the first shot.

When you've spent the years I had kicking around the world's trouble spots trying to stop it before it got out of hand, you know what kind of gun it is by the sound. The nine millimetre is a short cartridge with a distinctive cracking noise. No one in Dysant had a nine mm. No one shot the land for a mile in any direction without my permission—I owned it all. Anyone shooting would use a shotgun, which sounds very different.

My reaction was automatic. I moved for the desk drawer. The rule is, hear the shot, take evasive or retaliatory action and thank your God you heard it because that means it missed you. You never hear the one that hits you, and the one that writes finish to a brilliant career instantly is the one you don't hear or feel.

The L.G. cartridges were in the drawer. They contain six .36-calibre balls per cartridge, and I kept a box at Dysant because old Will Daniels was having trouble with the foxes. L.G. will cut a man in half at ten yards. I don't shoot any animals or birds unless I can kill painlessly. This is nothing to do with being humane. It's just respect for what you hunt. Finish your quarry instantly. I hope when I'm the quarry my hunter will return the compliment.

I told Mrs. Lewis we had poachers and she could tell her husband I would not be long. I went out the back very fast and made the high ground to the right of the cottage. I heard movement and saw a man staggering. He'd been through a rough time. He was dead on his feet, coughing his life's blood away. I know he was beyond help but tried to get to him before a man I could hear but not see beat me to him. Then the girl broke through the line of fir trees and ran toward the fallen man screaming "David, David."

I had one dead, one non-combatant to look out for, and didn't know where the opposition was. The book tells you sod the wounded, take cover, and take stock. But I've always had a soft spot for beautiful women, and killing unarmed civilian solicitors isn't playing the game, so I kept going. Then I saw the ape come up behind the girl and throw her to the ground. I was sixty yards away and out of effective range—the spread would have hit them both. So I kept on going.

I loved that ugly bastard for being a sadist, gloating over killing the girl as he walked backward from her so she could see death staring her in the face from the muzzle of the Colt automatic. Then I was fifteen yards away and knew she had less than a second to live when I let go two shots that rolled into one.

My first hit him on the right side and arm, spinning him so his back was to me. My second centred on his back and threw the bastard into the fir trees. Either blast would have killed him. You don't play heroes or give an opponent half a chance in a firefight.

I kept moving because there was trouble from my left. A second man thirty yards away was shooting—at me. My gun was empty and I had no chance to reload. If I stopped he'd turn his gun on the girl, and she'd be dead. Whatever anyone tells you, a running man is a difficult target to hit with a pistol. Yet he got close to me with one shot, because I felt the whiz near my face. But I was there and jumped across the girl shielding her. My opponent's gun had jammed and he threw it down, at the same time disappearing from sight behind the fir trees.

I stayed low to see if there were any more of the bastards. I reached down for the fallen Colt automatic, then reloaded the shotgun while I covered the girl—not an easy task. I didn't want her rushing about hysterically trying to revive her dead husband and providing anyone else with a good target. All I wanted to do was get the hell out of there because I didn't like the odds on protecting the girl and taking someone else out at the same time.

I heard the car start up and chanced kneeling to get a shot at it through a gap in the trees. My fugitive was driving the girl's white MGB at a range of one hundred fifty yards and opening. I saved the shot. The speed he was going, I'd be lucky to hit the hill behind him. I remember swearing, then felt the girl move.

I am not the world's best when it comes to dealing with hysterical women, and this one had gone off the deep end. I hadn't wanted her to see her husband lying there in some grotesque parody of death. I held her back but she kept coming at me, clawing, gouging, biting, kneeing, elbowing, a total attack. So I hit her a few times, which brought her back briefly to reality.

I half carried her to the cottage and laid her on the sofa. She was warm, quivering like a frightened animal. She was crying and staring into space, so I got some scotch down her. I lit two cigarettes, gave her one, and took a stiff slug of malt. So far it hadn't been a good day.

She was looking at me now, bewilderment and hate in her eyes. I hoped she wasn't going to get up and kick me in the groin again. I felt inadequate. How do you tell someone you were thinking bedroom thoughts about that you're sorry her husband's just been shot, even sorrier she had to see it, but you got one of the bastards and one day soon you'd get the other one? And that then the world would be right again and everlasting happiness would shine from the heavens? It never worked that way.

"Why did they kill him?" she demanded. "You must know—he was working for you."

Then she came at me again, in blind fury. She fought like a demented tigress who's just lost her cubs and has no reason to live. I hit her again. I wasn't proud of it but I had my reasons. A car was speeding down the driveway and I needed to know who was in it. So I threw her on the sofa and she curled into a heap crying again. I admired that girl. She was half crazy with grief but one hundred percent fight.

Grabbing the shotgun, I glanced out of the window. We weren't in the world's best defensive position but it was better than being caught in open ground, even with the potential fifth column on the sofa. I recognized the car. Some of the locals had sensed trouble when they found old Will Daniels unconscious in a ditch down the road. The pubs had barely been open an hour and it wasn't market day, so they knew he wasn't drunk. He had been hit very hard by a professional and ended up in intensive care. They had heard shots and put it down to my sporting activities, but when the white MGB came tearing up my driveway and forced an old van off the road, they thought I could be in trouble. They knew I didn't have a car so they formed a posse to investigate. In a gunfight they'd have been worse than useless but I admired their courage. They came piling out of the old Morris holding any kind of weapon they had at hand.

I went out and spoke to old Gwyn Trevor.

"Police and doctor, fast, Gwyn."

He raced for his van and drove off again. His two sons, fit, athletic lads, came running over.

"You all right Mr. Wyatt?"

"Yes. Come with me a minute."

They looked puzzled as I walked across to my desk, scribbled a message and a phone number on the pad, then gave it to them. Both looked at Mrs. Lewis, who lay crying on the sofa.

"Get to the nearest phone. Repeat that message to whoever answers. Both of you."

They ran across the woods toward Dysant. Mrs. Lewis tried to get up and this time she wasn't fighting. She ran for the kitchen and threw up. Then I put her back on the sofa, gave her a glass of water, and the cavalry started arriving.

A white cruise car, blue lights flashing, klaxon blaring. The first man out started to use his authority.

"Now then, who are you and—"

The second man charged into the cottage, looked at Mrs. Lewis and back at me.

"What—"

I finished up soldiering as a major, with a reputation for not suffering fools gladly and having one hell of a bad temper.

"You, stay with the lady," I interrupted the second man, then turned to the first.

"You, radio—with me.

"First, doctor and or ambulance. That woman is in shock. Next—"

He called in the first request.

"Next. Alert for white MGB registration X Ray Whisky November 93 Juliet. Do not approach occupant. May be armed. Will certainly kill."

"But—"

"Do it, laddie."

"Get your control to pass that on. That guy will travel. He just killed a man," I told him as he radioed.

"Advise your head of C.I.D."

"Are you a police officer or what, because—" the lad started to argue.

"Just do it. I tell him what happened. No one else."

I went back inside and saw Mrs. Lewis stammering out words to the second cop. He had his notebook out and was doing a good job. I went over to the desk, took a large whisky and unloaded the shotgun.

"You'll want this," I said. "Evidence."

The ambulance arrived, followed by a doctor who sedated Mrs. Lewis and put her on a stretcher. I stayed out of the way and went back to the desk where I started writing. More police cars arrived sporadically. Then the arrival of a helicopter touching down nearby caused a general stir. The three men running from it put the cops in a flat spin because my lads were carrying Heckler-Koch automatic rifles and looked like they knew what they were for.

"Nobody panic," I yelled. "They're the good guys."

The first man to the house was six foot four and seventeen stone of hard muscle. Dark hair was close cropped on top of what I can only call a disused quarry of a face further lined by a knife scar across the forehead. The other two men ignored the police and took up defensive positions around the outside of the cottage.

"You okay?" the big fellow demanded in a mid-European accent.

I nodded, then whistled. The two other men approached. The first of these was a stocky, Asian-looking individual with shiny black hair and a heavy, permanently smiling face, who wore an open-necked shirt and jeans. He was five foot tall, if that, but heavily built.

"Ko."

"Tuan." He smiled.

A police sergeant came over, a tall, authoritative, military-looking man in his mid-forties.

"What the hell is all this?"

"Rank and regiment," I snapped.

"Sergeant, 2 Para.," he automatically responded.

I didn't give him time to think.

"Wyatt, Major 22 S.A.S.," I replied. "Sergeant, go with Ko. Ko." I pointed. "Two men came in from the road on foot. Where they came from, where they hid the car, to where they shot a man beyond the cottage, to where I shot one."

"Tuan." He nodded.

"Sergeant." I cut him short from his objections. "Ko is a Dayak tracker. What he's doing here is a long story. Go with him, see what he finds. I'll clear it with your guv'nor. He'll go to the bodies first."

A posse of cops surrounded Ko, who led them to the back of the house and beyond. I heard him curse them in his native tongue for trying to go ahead of him. But he made himself understood.

By this time the police headman had arrived. He was a short, wiry, foxy-looking man called Caswell, and none too pleased at finding me in command, especially with all the artillery around. But I cooled him down, explained what had happened, and what I'd done already. Forensic men arrived and by the time I'd shown Caswell the bodies, there were police markers all over the place. Ko showed us the route the men had followed, how they'd come upon Lewis, where I had been. The forensic men didn't believe the signs Ko was reading from hard ground until I translated his explanations.

By 4:20 P.M. we'd covered it all. Caswell wanted me to stay available. It turned out he was ex-army, had done his bit in Cyprus, and understood my reasoning. Eventually he stopped treating me like a criminal. I suppose I could understand him doing that. It's the type of clientele policemen usually have.

We ended up liking each other, and we drank what was left of the scotch while puzzling out the motives for the crime. I didn't know, and that angered me.

Caswell discovered that David Lewis had left not only a widow but a daughter. One of Caswell's friends was a man named Roberts, who was in partnership with Lewis.

Then the police had gone and I was left with my three men.

The big fellow with the mid-European accent sat with me in the cottage. He had left Hungary in '56 after the uprising, with the K.G.B. hot on his tail. He'd soldiered for money around Africa for ten years. I met him in Jerusalem when he turned up fighting for a principle this time. We lost touch for a while until early '72 when I saw him again in London. I took him on as head of security for Aberinvest, which was growing. Two years later he fired himself from the job and took to following me around wherever I went. Shortly afterward any extremist idiot who wanted to make a name for himself took to sniping at politicians, industrialists, and prominent businessmen. Then the kidnappers started work and like it or not I was a target. I felt safer having the big man watch my back, and no one came near us. I'd never actually stopped paying him as head of security, so Aberinvest had two—one to do the job, the original to watch me. His name was unpronounceable—I'd always known him as Johnny. He was still alive, forty-six years old, drinking the last of the vodka, and worrying about me.

"I've told you to keep a telephone and a decent gun here," he grumbled.

"Johnny. I retired from business almost two years ago. No one knows who I am here. Hell, it's ten years since anyone shot at me."

"We're going to Cei Bach," he announced. "And you're coming."

I shook my head. I wanted time to think.

"There's three of us and one of you, Wyatt. I mean it."

He meant it. And he was right. I didn't fancy being felled like a pole-axed ox and bundled into the Sikorsky, so I walked. And in less than half an hour we touched down at Ty Newydd.

Chapter Ten

I had bought and extended Ty Newydd in the days I'd been playing the business game. The Victorian country house stood on twenty acres of its own ground, two miles from the coast. It was a secure establishment, the grounds crisscrossed with electronic surveillance cameras and closed-circuit television. We'd had most of Europe's top industrialists and politicians there at some time. We kept it secure because

Aberinvest used it for conferences, meetings, and as a weekend retreat. I was rarely there. Staffed by a housekeeper, the odd local help, four of my ex-soldiers, and several large agressive-looking dogs, Ty Newydd was probably the safest place to fort up while I tried to find out what was going on.

Mrs. Eluned Harries, my middle-aged, motherly, widowed housekeeper, greeted me like a long-lost son, took me into her kitchen and started cooking gammon and eggs, because I had obviously not been looking after myself properly at Dysant. She made me a pot of tea that would have revived a shocked elephant, told me not to smoke my thin Havanas in her kitchen, then relented because she thought I'd had a nasty experience.

"Mr. Wyatt, it's time you found a good woman to look after you and married her. Sam is a lovely girl. She can handle all your secretarial work and she can cook."

In her quaint Welsh way Mrs. Harries was trying to pair me off with my secretary. So I ribbed her.

"You two been conspiring against my freedom again?"

"You know very well Sam's not like that. She's never even mentioned you or your work or—"

"Is that gammon burnt?" I yelled. She turned quickly to look at the cooker, then threw a tea towel at me.

"For shame. Out of my kitchen."

All my lads are agreed you've got more chance against an Israeli battalion than Mrs. Harries, even when she's only playing angry.

My rooms are on the first floor at Ty Newydd. There's a large bedroom, a drawing room, bathroom, an executive office, and my study. I ate the gammon and eggs, washed the meal down with a mug of hot black coffee, and lit another Havana. I watched the closed-circuit screens covering the grounds and checked the alarm systems. All the hardware was duplicated in a security room in the basement, where there were two alternative power sources. If one system was knocked out, the other took over. To destroy all the alarm systems and visual surveillance, you had to take the basement, work your way around dozens of rooms, and find my study. Then you had to take out alarm systems there.

I lifted an internal phone and used words I hadn't spoken in ten years—since I'd left the army.

"Officers' call. My study in thirty minutes."

I sat back in the armchair and tried to put my thoughts together. Only in the quiet times, alone, do you realize how close you came to death. My hand was shaking ever so slightly. The meal had stopped my stomach bouncing up and down. I'd had little time to think, during the shooting, afterward when the police arrived, and on the flight back to Ty Newydd. Now there was nothing to organize, for the moment at least. So I took the day's events, one by one, and worked on them, with the aid of a notepad and pen.

David Lewis was to have called and given me a contract to sign on a straightforward land deal from a local estate that owed the taxman money. No reason for killers there. Lewis was a local solicitor, married, with a daughter. I couldn't see his family or clients hiring killers. Me, a man with an active record of involvement against terrorists, then the head of a multi-national corporation, then a semi-retired fisherman. Yes, there were possibilities. But they hadn't gone for me; they'd gone for Lewis. He hadn't got in their way. If he had, they'd probably have put him out, like Will Daniels. Unless he'd seen them, could identify them. Perhaps they were after me. But Ko's tracking scotched that possibility. Lewis had been to the house, seen my note, then gone into the woods for a walk, probably to use up some time. Ko had found two sets of tracks coming from the fields, across the wood, then stopping, crouching, obviously having seen Lewis. They had not gone near the house. They'd stalked Lewis for a good hundred yards, then one man had circled him. Lewis had run at the sound of the first shot, because Ko found a nine-mm shell case from the Colt automatic thirty feet from where Lewis had stood. Two more shell cases were found as one man had chased him back toward the house then fired twice. Lewis had kept going some way, dead on his feet. I knew the rest.

Unless they'd mistaken him for me.

I had this guilty feeling that I had something to do with Lewis' death. Because of me, a quiet family man who went about his business had been cut down by a pair of murderous hooligans. Because of me, a beautiful woman was crazy with grief and a child had lost her father.

I'd packed up soldiering at twenty-five. I'd gone into business with some money a grateful sheikh had given me for rescuing his son. There had been enough action and blood, enough bodies, wrecked communities, dead civilians. I'd seen my share of it, trying to keep places safe for everyone else to enjoy. The problem was they didn't realize they were losing the battle against terrorism even then. The only way to stop a terrorist is to invert his weapon of terror against him. Ethics and morality are the privileges of safe, civilized people dealing with each other. They don't apply when your enemy doesn't play by the rules.

I stopped being a businessman for other reasons. Maybe I didn't like myself doing the things you had to to make money. The fun was setting it all up, doing the deals, building up the companies. Then I realized I had all the money I'd ever need and it was like Monopoly and just as unreal. I had a lot of power and influence in places where it counted. Governments started to ask me to sit on various boards. My decisions affected the economies of countries, the lives of people, their environments. I mixed with the powerful, the affluent, the very influential. And soon I knew I was doing it for the sake of more power and influence. I'd become like everyone else up there. I couldn't give a moneky's about the people my actions affected.

So I handed over control to Peter Fallon, kept the title of non-executive chairman and a seat on the board. He'd got used to me over the seven years we'd been together, but I

70

wanted him to know that if he did take the trouble to locate me, I'd probably give him a good argument. If only out of pique at being disturbed.

I spent most of my time fishing and sometimes chasing beautiful women. Both activities have a healthy effect on a man, make him realize his failings. I loved West Wales, the peace, the countryside, the people. I took more interest in the farming side of Aberinvest and for the first time enjoyed trudging over fields, looking at stock, talking to farmers, and boozing in the pubs on market day.

But the gunfire had come back. The men of violence had been sent in. A man had died.

I was going to find out why.

They'd all assembled in the executive office. Johnny was looking out of the window, Gauloise hanging between his lips. Ko sat cross-legged on the floor. Next to him was Bill Grant, the third man who had come to Dysant. He was a Scot, my age, now married to a local girl and living two miles away in one of the estate cottages. Lack of work in his native Highlands had sent him soldiering after a boyhood spent on one of the sporting estates. He had joined me when his time was up and proved a first-class gamekeeper. He loved the land, and no one poached on Ty Newydd unless Bill turned a blind watchful eye. Ko acted as his assistant.

Frank Price was a local man. I'd met him in the army. Forty years old now, lean, tall, tough as tank armour, an ex-sergeant without equal. First-rate explosives man, sniper, communications specialist, he now took charge of security at Ty Newydd. Under him he had Tom Watson, former paramedic and survival specialist, who was watching the electronics and not present.

I told the story, asked for any suggestions, and put the place on maximum alert. Johnny advised Jack Morgan, the farm's manager, and his son Graham, who ran the estate stables. So everyone knew.

"We don't know who or what or why. Maybe it's not me

someone's after but I'm in, come what may. Anyone wants out, speak now.''

I was greeted by silence.

''Bill, pass the word to all civilians employed. No one's to go playing silly buggers if they see anyone or anything unusual, no heroics. Leave that to the pros among us. Understood?''

Everyone nodded. Then I was alone with Johnny.

''You're going sentimental,'' he observed, pouring me a malt whisky. I lit another thin Havana and retreated into my study.

''You spent half an hour up here on your own. Your damn conscience is playing you up. You're thinking about today, telling yourself it must be your fault. You can't get the woman out of your mind, can you?''

I shook my head.

''That's what I thought.'' He swallowed his drink, turned on his heel.

''Where are you going?'' I asked.

''Clean my gun,'' he replied. ''If you're in that frame of mind, someone's in trouble.''

Samantha came in twenty minutes later. She had been shopping in Cardigan. Mrs. Harries had obviously been gossiping about all the activity because Sam threw her arms round me and kissed me.

Sam has long brown hair, long legs, wide hazel eyes, and a slender figure. She is twenty-two years old, fiercely independent, a believer in women's rights, and a first-rate personal assistant. She understands computer operations, all modern business gadgetry, and how to get her way with me, most of the time. She lives at Ty Newydd in her own rooms and some of the time sleeps in mine.

I disentangled myself, slapped her backside, and pointed to the office.

''Work,'' I ordered, taking my glass with me.

''We're in trouble, I take it.''

''Possibly.''

I gave her a two-minute résumé of events and told her to send for Jennings, one of our P.R. men who lived in Swansea. He was to call and see Arthur Roberts, Lewis' partner, who I understood from Caswell was looking after the widow and daughter. I told him not to offend anyone, but to make sure that Mrs. Lewis received the best medical attention and to take care of any funeral expenses, accommodation, whatever. Maybe I was ducking out by sending the hired help, but today I could not face grieving survivors and stand idly by with no answers.

Sam tried to locate Peter Fallon, who, it turned out, was in Paris. We didn't raise him until he called me at midnight about a woman who was camping on his doorstep, demanding to see me about a matter of vital importance. She gave no name or indication of why she wanted to see me and refused to speak to me on the telephone. Fallon had her down as being sensible, levelheaded, and very earnest, so I told him to get her down early next morning.

I wasn't taking any chances. I sent Johnny and Ko to watch over Mrs. Lewis from a discreet distance, just in case the police weren't. They were told to stay out of sight. Bill and Tom Watson would relieve them at midnight, so everyone could get some sleep.

I kept thinking about Lewis and whether the connection with the land purchase really was a line of inquiry I could discount. Sir Nigel Appleton had instructed him; Appleton was the man to contact. He was not pleased about being disturbed at dinner, and Sam sweetly turned his wrath in my direction.

"Wyatt, can't a man eat in peace?"

"David Lewis can't. He's dead. Someone shot him."

"You're not serious." Appleton was genuinely horrified. But then he would regard lawyers as a protected species.

"One line of thought is this land deal."

"Absolutely not. It's the Tremynach Estate you're dealing with, not Al Capone."

"When did you see him?" I asked.

"Tuesday lunchtime, at Romulus, after—"

"After what, Nigel?"

"A busy morning, followed by a hectic afternoon. What do the police say?"

"At last sight, not a lot. You've no thoughts, then?"

"No, sorry."

Which did not seem true. I wondered what he had been doing Tuesday morning. Was the distinguished Sir Nigel Appleton telling me little white lies? Or was my suspicious mind working too hard?

I waited up till after midnight for Johnny and Ko to come back. There was press activity outside the Lewis house earlier. The police in attendance were keeping them at bay. No one else had been near the place, except Jennings. A man and woman were staying at the house with Mrs. Lewis and her daughter.

So I sat alone for a while, in the study, with a balloon or two of Armagnac as the only company I wanted. I wondered what Fallon's woman visitor wanted. Perhaps that would have some bearing. About one-thirty I rolled in the direction of my bedroom, not totally sober, and found Samantha lying on my bed, attired in my silk dressing gown.

"Hi," she smiled, arching one long leg.

"Just going to wash away the smell of cordite." I pointed to the shower.

The hot water had the desired soothing effect. I came out of the shower and Sam was there holding a towel.

"I'll rub your back for you."

"Thanks."

"What's that?" She stroked a mark on my collar bone.

"War wound," I joked.

"Seriously."

"Only scratch I ever received in combat, ducking under an Arab's knife. You can hardly see it now."

"Poor Wyatt." She kissed the offended shoulder. "And now they're shooting at you again."

She put her arms around my waist and kissed the other shoulder, then worked her way round me. The dressing gown slid off her shoulders to the floor. She moved her pelvis into me and her pert breasts pressed into my chest. I kissed her and lifted her off her feet.

"What a strong Wyatt you are." She kept kissing and biting my earlobes. I carried her into the bedroom and lowered her gently onto the circular bed. She took my left arm and suddenly jerked it against the elbow joint, judo throwing me next to her on the bed. The move took me by complete surprise as she landed on my chest, knees pressing on my shoulders. The long hair fell down toward me as she smiled.

"Got you, boyo." She laughed, her arms outstretched, trying to pin my arms flat.

"I'm not fighting," I confessed.

"Good. Ever been raped?"

I shook my head. Then she kissed me, kneeling, legs astride my waist.

"This is how it's done, Major."

Chapter Eleven————————————————

I woke at seven, feeling the effects of a little too much brandy and a lot too much Sam. So I showered, shaved, went into my study, and rang for breakfast, which was more gammon and eggs, toast, black coffee.

Johnny reported at eight-thirty that the Sikorsky with Fallon on board was in the air and in radio contact. He helped himself to coffee and lit a Gauloise.

"You look dreadful, Wyatt. Can't you get that girl to leave you alone?"

"Why?" I asked, faking innocence.

"Because I'm going to London for a day or two," he replied. "Look up some old friends and find out who's been spreading money around to have people hit. The boys'll keep an eye on you. Just stay indoors, out of sight."

He had that look on his face again, the one that said I'm not advising you, I'm telling you. So I told him about my phone call to Appleton, and the way my thoughts had run.

"Sounds logical," he agreed. "But we need information. I'll have to look for it."

"Who looks out for Mrs. Lewis? We're spreading ourselves a bit thin."

"You sure we aren't watching her just because she's a good-looking broad and her husband's out of the way?"

He caught my angry expression.

"Sorry—that was nasty. I didn't mean it, Wyatt," he apologized.

"You may be right," I told him. "That woman is difficult to forget."

"I told you, you're going sentimental. You're at a dangerous age when it comes to women. It didn't matter in the old days. A screw was just a screw and what the hell—it could be the last one you had. Then you started being a tycoon. A screw was still just a screw because you had to win all the deals, buy the world. Now you've begun to live like a human being, not a killing machine or a mobile bank balance and you suddenly find that people matter, women especially. It's not the chase that interests you or the capture, it's what happens afterward and you don't realize it."

I poured more coffee.

"You're being very profound today, Johnny."

"Just remember, you're not twenty anymore. If we do go looking for trouble and find it, remember two things. One, the kids today are better than they were, better trained, better armed, and bloody fanatics. Two, you throw down on a target and think for a split second that's a human being, especially if it's a woman, and you've made your last mistake. Time was you'd have had both those bastards you met yesterday for breakfast. You only got one. Well, I had my say. Just think about it, eh?"

He put the coffee cup back on my desk.

"I'll go back with the chopper after you've seen that woman Fallon's bringing."

The door closed behind him. I thought about his advice. True friends are people who'll die for you and happen rarely in a lifetime, if at all. Johnny was an employee, but he was a friend first. He rarely gave advice. When he did, the advice was important.

The Sikorsky arrived at nine-thirty and Fallon came straight up to my study. He was slim, five six, thirty-two years old, with close-cut blond hair, bright blue eyes and a youthful, almost boyish face that had the women falling over him. He dressed in modern Italian-style three-piece suits, silk shirts, and Gucci shoes. The ties were on the loud side. He put his briefcase in the outer office and shook hands with a grip that felt boneless but fooled you.

"You been upsetting people again," he joked.

"Somebody shoots and kills our lawyer. Then this lady wants to talk to me. What do you make of your travelling companion?"

"For a lady as sensible, levelheaded, articulate, and intelligent as she is to be camping out at my flat, she has a problem. There's no melodrama about it. She wants to tell you, and no one else. What this lady wants I think you'll find she gets."

Five minutes later I was alone in the study with a conservatively dressed blond lady in her early forties who seemed unsure of herself. I watched the green eyes look directly into mine, then around the room.

"Do sit down." I offered her the armchair and a cigarette which she accepted the way a nervous occasional smoker does.

"Thank you, Major Wyatt."

Which should have been the first clue. Apart from Fallon and the Ty Newydd crowd, my military background wasn't known to many people. There was something vaguely familiar about the woman. I was sure I'd seen her somewhere.

"What can we do for you, Mrs.—?"

She left my invitation to give her name in the air. I felt slightly uncomfortable. I like to know who I'm dealing with. Then she became very businesslike, as if the uncertainty had been overcome and she was embarking on a do-or-die attempt at something.

"You probably won't remember me. We have not met for some years. I've come to you because you're certainly the last chance I have. I don't know whether I can trust you, but I have to. If I've made a mistake, Sir Philip Moresby has no hope."

When she mentioned Philip Moresby, I recalled where I'd seen her: in the Ministry of Defence.

"What's old Philip been up to, Mrs. Burton?"

"He's been arrested for espionage."

That sounded as probable as the Pope being caught in a brothel. It wasn't April Fool's Day. I wasn't drunk. And the lady didn't strike me as being some kind of practical joker.

"This isn't one of Philip's party games, is it? 'I am going to Washington for the weekend, so make up a cover story for me while I'm away'?"

She shook her head. I lit a Havana and watched her for a while. Then I flipped open an address book, reached for an outside telephone, and dialled a number. A Ministry telephonist answered.

"Mrs. Burton, please, Special Services."

I waited four seconds. A woman's voice answered.

"Mrs. Burton, please."

"I'm afraid Mrs. Burton is on leave. Who is this—?"

I put the phone down. She looked very relieved.

"I thought you were going to tell someone I was here," she confessed.

"Tell me more, Mrs. Burton."

So I had the story. On Monday morning, Moresby had been arrested by M.I.5 and taken for interrogation. She had been interviewed, and later warned off communicating with anyone, by a man called Llewellyn Jones. She was not to leave London unless she advised a certain Quittenden of S.I.S. She had been refused access to Moresby and I was the only help she could think of. She didn't know whether I'd laugh, turn her in, or even listen. But she had gambled. And now sat there waiting for my reaction.

"You do realize, Major, that the whole security system will be concentrating on breaking Sir Philip, and anyone else who becomes involved."

So I drew on my Havana, and watched her again for a while.

"That's life, Mrs. Burton. No one said it was meant to be easy."

"You'll help?"

"I'll try. Meanwhile, you stay here. If anyone's watching you, they'll know you've gone. And if you go back, there'll be some very awkward questions. I know very little about security operations, so you'll have to advise me on who's who and what's what."

I had Sam conduct Mrs. Burton to the guest wing and make sure she was comfortable while I dialled Sir Philip Moresby's home number. I got the unobtainable signal and then spent five minutes trying to reach him. Eventually an operator answered. After twenty more minutes the operator called me back and told me the number was no longer in use. Nothing unusual in that, expect that Philip Moresby had changed his number on two previous occasions and each time he had called me the same day to give me the new number.

The alarm light above number three closed-circuit camera flashed red. Instantly Frank Price's voice came through on my desk console.

"Intruders, Wyatt. Red sector. Two men."

I could see them on the screen. They were in the grounds,

having scaled a ten-foot wall that ran through the Morfa Wood at the west end of the estate. They were four hundred yards from the house. They'd taken good enough care to screen themselves from the house but not from the cameras.

"Check all other sectors," I snapped back, then pressed another button on the desk.

"Ko, cut off their retreat. Frank—dogs."

Johnny was in the study in less than two minutes, a Heckler-Koch rifle in his hands. I moved for the gun cabinet on the wall and took out my own FN CAL.

"Stay out of sight," Johnny ordered. "Could be a diversion."

Then he was gone. I lit a Havana, pulled back the cocking handle of the CAL, and watched the screens.

They were both young men, moving like trained infantry. They wore civilian clothes, but in the right colours for scouting: brown and green. Each had a pair of binoculars. Every move forward they made committed them further. I couldn't see our lads moving. I didn't expect to. Otherwise, it would be a pointless exercise.

They heard the dogs and rose, as if to run back the way they'd come. But they were flanked by Johnny and Frank Price, who had a shotgun levelled at them. They looked at each other, then at the two Alsatians, fangs properly bared, and decided it was time to give in. They assumed the prone position, and Frank chucked his shotgun to Johnny before searching them. Finally he snapped handcuffs on them and brought them in.

There was no harm in letting them see some of the setup, so I had them brought up to the study where Sam was serving me more coffee. They had little to say to anyone, but the first, a tall, dark-haired lad of twenty-five or so, made a very improper suggestion to Sam.

"Little boys who are caught scrumping apples don't interest me." She smiled sweetly and walked out. Johnny grinned as he sat them in two chairs. Frank Price put a bundle of items on the desk in front of me. There were two nine-mm Browning automatic pistols, some money, a couple of hand-kerchiefs, cigarettes. But no wallets, driving licences, credit cards, or any form of identification.

"They don't want to say anything," Johnny advised me.

I looked at the faces, lean, tanned faces with quiet eyes that just stared back at me. They'd had a good look around the room and doubtless everything they had passed on the way up.

"Shoot them," I ordered. Then the looks they exchanged weren't quite so confident. I walked over to the window while Johnny hauled them to their feet. Then they made their move. The taller one kicked out at Johnny, who took the kick on a cross-handed guard and flattened his opponent. The shorter man charged at me, head low. I sidestepped, and he caught his head on the wall. He was down and out. Johnny hauled the first man up again. He was winded, but gasped out, "Bloody well do it, then."

Johnny threw him back in his chair and collected his com-panion from under my feet. The second man wasn't going to wake up for quite some time. The thud of his head on the wall had been quite sickening. I lifted the telephone.

"Sam. Get me a fellow called Caswell."

The first man was now looking at me again.

"Very impressive," he breathed hard. "But you might as well shoot. I won't be saying anything." I ignored him and spoke to Johnny.

"They'll take any creampuff in the S.A.S. these days."

Now you can beat hell out of them, torture them, threaten to kill them. You can starve them, you can ignore them, you can disorient them. They'll just look at you and clam up. It's part of the training. But I've yet to meet an S.A.S. man who'll take an insult to himself or the regiment without giving you some kind of reaction, however well-disguised. This one was better than most, but I caught the flash in his eyes. If Johnny had turned him loose, he'd have killed me.

"Relax," I invited. "You two are perfectly safe. Do you want a cigarette?"

The man shook his head.

"Pointless asking who sent you, or why. If you do know, I'd get nothing out of you. So while we wait for the —"

My phone rang.

"Caswell, this is Wyatt. We've just caught two armed men in the grounds here. No panic, they're rendered safe. Can you come over?"

"On my way."

"Sorry," I apologized to my intruder. "While we wait for the police I'll tell you a story. Once upon a time there was a man who'd been around, knew the way the game was played, made a lot of money, bought all this. Then he retired and minded his own business and enjoyed fishing. He went to a place of peace and quiet where the people were ordinary and friendly. Then one day somebody started shooting at a lawyer who worked for him, killed the lawyer, and shot at the man. The man wondered why. Then the man heard about something rotten in the state of the security system. Two large, aggressive, armed persons came calling, and the man wondered why. So he decided to find out what was going on. And he was the kind of man who found out what he wanted to know. He was very wealthy, had a lot of influence, and knew how to use it. He wasn't frightened by guns and conspiracies and the nastier forms of life. Are you following the story?"

Our captive nodded.

"Then go and tell whoever sent you," I instructed.

Detective Chief Superintendent Caswell gave me a foxy look and lit a Capstan Full Strength. His glass of whisky was getting close to empty, so I refilled it. His men had removed our two visitors an hour before. He'd taken a phone call in my study, looked hard at me, and put the receiver down. He looked at my signed statement that lay on my desk.

"You aren't telling me something, Wyatt."

He had that cop look again, the one that says I don't know what's going on. You do. Start telling.

"Such as?"

"You've made a complaint of armed trespass against two unnamed men. They're not in my custody longer than twenty minutes when I get a phone call from my chief constable. Someone in London with a lot of clout says let them go. They are on a top-level security investigation. I think you know."

"I've met their type before," I admitted.

"You've mixed with them. Friend of mine in the Met. told me all about you. Now my chief is thinking about arresting you for the manslaughter of a Mad Jack Bannion, one-time I.R.A. man. He's thinking about adding wasting police time. Maybe I'll have my firearms officer come down here and check the certificates for all this obvious hardware. Perhaps I'll run you in under prevention of terrorism or something."

"I know a newspaper man who'd be interested to hear you say that," I replied. "Constitutes what I call threatening behaviour."

"You mean the three newspapers you own in Europe would come to your aid?"

"Deal, Caswell. I tell you what I know. Then you cough."

He looked hard at me, then gave me a sly grin.

"I don't discuss police business."

"And I don't like being shot at."

It was standoff time. He was trying to make up his mind whether to trust me when the telephone rang. Someone called Llewellyn Jones from London wanted to talk. I left the call on the desk speaker so Caswell could hear. I'd made up my mind about him, to a point. He had to decide about me.

"Wyatt," I said.

The voice on the other end sounded political. The tone was persuasive and the accent very faintly Welsh.

"Mr. Wyatt. My name is Llewellyn Jones. I wonder if you could come and see me tomorrow at the Home Office? Very vital matter to discuss that I'd rather not talk about over the phone."

"Sorry I'm tied up all week. Shall we say next Tuesday?"

"I'd rather it were tomorrow. Shall we say twelve-thirty. Then I can give you lunch."

"If you say so," I replied.

"I shall look forward to it. Good morning, Mr. Wyatt."

He put the telephone down. Sam came in with an open copy of *Who's Who*. Llewellyn Jones was a very senior civil servant.

"Caswell, I received information this morning that a very senior person has been arrested for espionage. Now we've all breached the Official Secrets Act. I reckon the two goons you had worked for the security boys. They wanted to know what I was doing."

"How senior is this person?" Caswell asked.

"About as high as you can go."

"Listen to me, Wyatt. I'm not telling you this because you've got clout, I'm telling you because I think you're straight. The man you shot was an ex-I.R.A. thug called Bannion with a track record as a professional killer—nothing proven, nevertheless a killer. From Mrs. Lewis' statement and identification I believe that the second man was also a killer, a Lebanese named Nury al Said. Now when I ask Special Branch for information I find a block. Then my chief constable has a phone call. Nury al Said is required by the Security Services and I am to lay off. I can go through the motions, and then drop it. Within a week, someone will make up a story that Said has cleared the country and can't be found. The press will be happy with my incredible detection and not so happy with international police cooperation. I'm being leaned on."

"And I suspect that the call from the Home Office is a summons so they can do likewise on me."

"We have a problem," Caswell observed after some thought.

84

"You might have. I want justice and some answers. Cheers."

Caswell raised his glass.

"Keep in touch." He gathered my statement forms. "Let's see what my chief will do about this. And Wyatt—be careful."

Chapter Twelve

Second Assistant Secretary Vladimir Baikal's brow furrowed into a puzzled expression. His heavy hand reached for a cigarette from the box on his desk. Walking to the window of the Embassy annex, he looked out over Kensington Palace Gardens. He was of medium height, stocky build with the heavy face and deliberate movements of a bear. Balding, thirty-five, he unfortunately looked like what he was—an expert in causing the more physical kind of trouble. The Embassy listed him as a second assistant secretary with responsibility for trade. His real function was head of the Disinformation section of London's K.G.B. station.

He enjoyed the posting and hoped for promotion. Washington was his next goal. Yet he stood reviewing his past performance and worrying. Two hours before, he had received a signal from Moscow Centre. Have a car and two good men at Heathrow by 1500 Thursday, August 26, for escort duty to the Embassy. No reason given, no names mentioned. The Ambassador had been no help. He was too busy ensuring his staff had prepared a room, the best room.

Baikal looked at the clock. It was now 1540. The car had returned ten minutes before. His men had not reported back. He paced the room, deliberately. He should have been informed of the visitor's arrival and identity. But he had not. There was cause for concern. Who the hell was visiting London?

Ten minutes later he was summoned by the Ambassador. Fifteen minutes later, he walked into the Green Room. The heavy velvet curtains were drawn. At the end of the room a tall man stood with his back to the door. The man turned and Baikal was aware of deep blue eyes penetrating him like a laser beam.

The man, fifty-five, was six foot three, and elegantly dressed. More like a French president than a Russian, Baikal thought. The long face had the deathly pallor of grey chalk, the lines and hollow cheeks and the thin frame that barely weighed eleven stone gave Baikal the impression of a walking cadaver.

Not a man easily frightened or shocked, Baikal's legs felt weak, his stomach empty. But he recovered quickly and stood at attention in front of General Alexei Svetkin, number-two man in Moscow Centre, deputy head of the K.G.B.

"General, an honour," he spoke firmly.

"Comrade, if you please, Vladimir Andreyevitch," Svetkin spoke, his voice deceptively soft, Baikal thought, worrying about the reason for Svetkin's visit. Never before had the General visited London.

"You are surprised to see me?" Svetkin raised his glass of Napoleon brandy.

"Yes, General—Comrade."

"Sit down, Vladimir Andreyevitch; help yourself to a brandy."

There was one consolation for Baikal. He had never been offered the Ambassador's best Napoleon before.

"British Intelligence is aware of my arrival," Svetkin announced. "I am here on business. You will place your men at my disposal, under my direct orders. You will continue with your normal duties as if I were not here; is that understood?"

"Perfectly, Comrade."

"Excellent. I shall use the Yellow Room."

Baikal looked puzzled, and worried. Short of nuclear war there was only one reason for the Yellow Room to be used—a crisis

Intelligence operation directed by and from Centre itself. The Yellow Room had a computer and direct communications link to Centre and all other stations, and telephone lines whose numbers were known only to Centre. No security staff was authorized to approach the room, except for visiting communications officers who had access for maintenance purposes only. Baikal could not recall a Yellow Room ever being used in his fifteen years of K.G.B. service.

"Comrade Vladimir Andreyevitch, don't look so worried. We are not expecting nuclear war. And your service to date has been adequate. We are not yet thinking of replacing you."

Baikal felt relief. Maybe Svetkin was not the monster he was reputed to be. He spoke quite softly, reassuringly even. But when he looked at Svetkin's eyes, the relief turned to apprehension. Those eyes had never left Baikal since he entered the room.

Simon Quittenden was advised of the new arrival to London by the duty M.I.5 officer at Heathrow. He sent for Richard Lansbury, who arrived in time for the second afternoon tea round at four-thirty.

"You've heard, I take it."

Lansbury puffed on his pipe and accepted the offer of a chair.

"My lads have got the Embassy under surveillance. Svetkin hasn't moved."

"Have you got anything going on that would warrant his attention?"

"I've never had anything that big," Lansbury admitted. "So what are my instructions?"

"Keep watch. If he moves, follow him, but not too closely."

"Any reason?" Lansbury inquired.

"He's an old hand. I don't want to frighten him off."

"Can you tell me why a police request for information and whereabouts of a Nury al Said was blocked by you?" Lansbury asked. He wanted to put Quittenden in the position of wondering how much he knew. But Quittenden suddenly became open.

"Yes. He killed a man called Lewis, who was given documents by Sir Nigel Appleton, who in turn had received information from Sir Philip Moresby. We don't want the Welsh Rangers putting their big feet in the soup. My department is now seeking Nury al Said abroad.''

"I see. So it's to do with Moresby. Escape route?''

Quittenden lit a cigarette and regarded Lansbury quizzically. Suddenly his expression changed to a smile. An instinct told Lansbury Quittenden had been acting out a charade for his benefit.

"Why should I tell you?''

"Because I was there when Calladyne pulled Moresby in. You gave me the feeling the other day that you suspected my motives in not mentioning something Moresby told me about meeting Colonel Fahd. I want to know where I stand. This whole operation is really a Five job, my job. But I don't get a look in. The office boy is better informed than me.''

Lansbury realized he had gone too far. Anger had loosened what should have been a cautious tongue. Quittenden was smiling again. Lansbury had the feeling that Quittenden had won the mental game of chess before Lansbury even realized it had begun.

"You worked with Moresby at S.S.D. for a time, didn't you?''

"Did twelve months with him back in seventy, liaison mostly and internal security.''

"Ever meet a man called Wyatt?''

"Big businessman now. Haven't seen him since early seventy-one. In those days he was a mad bastard.''

"Really.''

"Go anywhere. He pulled the Sheikh of Basquoos' rich little son right out from under two hundred P.L.O. There were five on his side. Only man I know equally welcome in Tel Aviv and Riyadh. Specialist in raids, small mobile teams. Always gets in and out fast.''

"Thanks for the commercial.'' Quittenden's expression changed.

"Why do you ask?"

"Lewis was on his way to see Wyatt when he was killed by Said."

"Wouldn't like to be Said then." Lansbury lit his pipe.

"Do something for me," Quittenden ordered. "Go and have a chat with Moresby. See if you can find out why Lewis went to see Wyatt."

Lansbury nodded. The interview was over. As he walked along Lancaster Gate, Richard Lansbury tried to work it all out. Is Quittenden setting me up, using me, or ignoring me? Or is it a combination of all three?

Quittenden knew exactly what he was doing. So did Alexei Svetkin. Both men sat simultaneously in the same city making inquiries of a network of agents worldwide regarding the whereabouts of Nury al Said.

Said was running. He had bribed an acquaintance of his to hide him on a cross-channel ferry bound for Ostend. Using one of several false passports he held, he appeared to Belgian customs as one of the many students disgorged from the 5 A.M. ferry to start hitchhiking and camping holidays. He had hitched his way through Belgium quickly and arrived at the frontier post at Givet in a French container-wagon. Bored French frontier guards waved the vehicle through without bothering to stamp Said's passport. From Reims, Said hitched another lift, which took him as far as Nantes. At Basle, he crossed the Swiss frontier illegally and took a train. By midday on Friday, August 27, he was sunning himself on the lakeside at Lugano, holiday resort of Ticino, Switzerland. He had some time to waste. The next stage of his journey was arranged. But the passport and travel timetable would take a while longer to materialize.

Quittenden had other problems. Mrs. Burton seemed to have disappeared. She had stayed in her flat all Tuesday before leaving sometime on Wednesday. Quittenden did not know at what time because the man detailed to watch her flat had become distracted by a girl walking an Alsatian. He had stopped her by way of a comment about the Alsatian and then casually remarked he lived in the area and had never seen the girl before. Quittenden would have given him full marks for casual interrogation technique and infiltration. He gave the watcher zero for observation, and a ten-minute lecture on attention to duty. Since the man was not from S.I.S. but on loan from Special Branch he did not take any notice and suggested in future Quittenden use his own men. The unfortunate transgressor was purging his contempt in a collators' office, shuffling records around.

For the two men dispatched to penetrate and observe Ty New-ydd and plant electronic surveillance equipment, Quittenden had fifteen minutes reserved—ten to listen to excuses and learn, five to deliver a reprimand. The ex-S.A.S. man and his by-now conscious colleague were returned to M.I. 5 plumbers' room with a sharp reminder that they had blown their cover, alerted the local police, and could have landed the department in political hot water if the house's occupants had pressed home the armed trespass charge.

But Simon Quittenden was not a man to worry unduly about setbacks. He had his case building. He had his agents set to find Nury al Said. And he was waiting for Mrs. Burton to surface. His money was on her going to seek help. The airports and seaports were being watched, and the police had by now received a nationwide alert to observe and report immediately, but not to apprehend.

So he fed more information into his computer, then lay on his camp bed, staring at the plain white ceiling, and tasting the victory of his new omnipotent position.

Chapter Thirteen

We fixed up the details during the helicopter flight to London. It was provocation time, and see who moved. By now it was obvious that Moresby's arrest was causing consternation, political and domestic. Someone didn't want Mrs. Burton talking to anyone. There had been no press release of any kind. I had two problems. One—who killed David Lewis? Two—what the hell had happened for Philip Moresby to get himself arrested? The thought fleetingly crossed my mind that the two incidents were interconnected, but I dismissed that. So we had to look at the Moresby problem.

I'd told Fallon the story about Moresby. Now Fallon is the best when it comes to Dow Jones, cash flow, forward projections, and the money supply. He is a first-rate economic theorist and can spot a winner in any financial field before the race has started. But he thinks security is the collateral you put up for a loan and that espionage is some competitor trying to nick your ideas before you've had a chance to turn them into money. His financial upbringing is so thorough that for years he thought Ian Fleming wrote economic textbooks about convertible securities.

But he knows everyone who is anyone.

"So I bump into the Attorney General and say—a pity about old Moresby. Still, more Reds under the bed must be embarrassing. I suppose you'll have to prosecute."

"You get the drift," I replied.

"After which I'm thrown out on my ear."

"Precisely. But then the Establishment knows we know. And if the Attorney General doesn't tell someone who translates this information into action against us, then we're fairly sure that they won't be prosecuting, and Moresby is in real trouble."

"Then I'm collected by heavy men and given the lights in the face treatment."

"So you casually mention my name," I proposed.

"And we're both given the lights in the face treatment," he countered.

"So have a battery of lawyers and a pile of pressmen standing by. So if they do come to get you, it'll be on 'News at Ten' and I'll know about it."

"You're serious."

"Indeed," I replied.

"You're mad."

"He's mad," Johnny agreed, "but it's a good first move."

By five-thirty, Johnny and I had occupied the executive flat at the top of Aberinvest's office building. Security on the entire building is tight. The flat is more of a penthouse avant-garde furniture exhibition than somewhere to live, but there were three double bedrooms, each with bathroom, an open plan kitchen with enough food to give Fortnum and Mason competition, and two superb living areas with space-age television, stereos, plants, and air conditioning. The cocktail cabinet was more of a bar recessed in a corner and contained everything except draught beer.

I settled on a lounging unit that would have done justice to Nero and contemplated a large malt. Johnny was contemplating a secretary who had brought groceries and the scent of Chanel No. 5 into the room. You wouldn't think an ugly old man like Johnny, who has a personality akin to scarified granite and the charm of a driverless juggernaut, could chat the women, but his record can beat anything anyone's ever notched up in Wisden. I remember a week's leave in Tel Aviv, when he was on a cricket score by the time I'd broken the duck.

She was cute, about twenty, five three, with pixie-cut brown hair and enormous blue eyes. She wore a blouse and skirt that seemed to split endlessly, and she moved around the room very quietly. When she'd finished Johnny insisted on pouring her a drink. She looked in my direction uncomfortably.

"Don't worry about him," Johnny quipped. "He's already in love."

"I'm not paid to sit around drinking," she admonished him.

"You are now," I commented.

Johnny steered her over in my direction, sat her down on another of the lounging units and told her she had the bluest eyes he'd ever seen. He gave her the biggest gin and tonic I'd ever seen. When the phone rang, she moved instinctively to answer it, but I held up my hand to tell her I could walk as well. I found the instrument disguised as a nineteenth-century door handle and spoke into it. Fallon was on the other end. He was to meet the Attorney General for a drink at six-thirty in Fallon's club. From there he would return to his Mayfair flat where I would meet him; no later than eight, no earlier.

No sooner had I put the phone down than Sir Nigel Appleton's secretary called me. Sam had given her my whereabouts because she knew I wasn't happy with my previous conversation. I asked if he could call at the penthouse in person at nine-thirty. This seemed acceptable.

When I looked round the girl had gone. Her name was Felicity—Latin for happiness—and having seen her I could believe it. Johnny was smiling like a cat that's tasted the cream and knows he's going to get a gallon of it very soon. He told me he was out to see some old friends and would meet me in Fallon's flat at seven-thirty. I was ordered to be careful and not go anywhere alone.

Which seemed like good advice. So I finished the scotch, went into the kitchen, grilled myself a rump steak and tossed some salad. I laid off the booze, sampled the Malvern water instead and knew why no one went there for the cure any-more. I kept thinking about Philip Moresby and what kind of food they were giving him, if any. I wondered what widows ate, how long they cried, and whether their children ever adjusted. I listened to a news' program, didn't like the world very much and longed to be fishing the Falls pool at Dysant. Then I told myself you can't duck your responsibilities. I could walk away, of course, say sod everyone, climb into the executive jet, and go anywhere for as long as I wanted. But if I did that, I'd still be wondering how long widows cried, what happened to my friend Moresby, and whether children ever adjusted.

Whichever way I looked at the problems they were down to me. Their solution frightened me. The means to their solution worried me. They were not going to be solved on any intellectual plane. They required action, and the kind of action I'd seen over the last two days meant somebody winding up dead. The problems could overwhelm me. But I've always had this stubborn, egotistical belief. The bastards might get me, but I'd have them, even if it was with a last reflex.

I met Johnny at Fallon's flat at seven forty-five. He started on the tonic water, which is a sure sign he's working, and stood at the side of the window.

"What do you know?" I asked.

"Some," he replied, eyes watching the street. "Bannion and Said have worked together before. They dropped out of sight Wednesday. This guy Said is a real nasty—likes hurting women. Bannion just liked hurting everyone. Word is the spooks are looking for Said."

"Which spooks?"

"Nobody said. Nobody wants to know."

"Who's after Moresby?"

"I've only got one pair of hands. My émigré chums say that a big K.G.B. man's hit town. But then so has a godfather, four soldiers, and a French contract man called Defarge. There's also a bunch of Irish nutters on the loose and Special Branch are everywhere. Take your pick—Here comes Fallon.''

Fallon parked his Porsche, locked it, and crossed the mews. Further down the road an Escort 2000, with two up, pulled into the kerb. Fallon lives in the type of Mayfair mews where anyone not driving a Rolls, Porsche, Aston Martin, or Mercedes is definitely slumming. He'd picked up a tail.

Fallon came in, shut the door, and headed straight for the Armagnac.

"I did as my master requested," he announced. "Poured claret down old Jeremy, made the right noises."

"And what happened?"

"Felt like being up before the headmaster. I started with a pity about poor old Moresby and all that. Jeremy gave me one of his blank stares, which is his usual way of covering up. Does it in the Commons all the time. Then he asked whether Philip had got Montezuma's revenge or something because the last he'd heard Philip was in Acapulco. So I plodded on and said pull the other leg and all hell broke loose."

As Fallon defined all hell, I could see Johnny was amused.

"I was told to go back to running multi-nationals, to leave such matters to the proper authorities, and stop using the old pals act to embarrass old chums. If I didn't keep my mouth shut consequences would be unpleasant."

"Such as?" I asked.

"He hinted very broadly that certain ministries would dream up reasons for investigating certain companies. There would be press leaks and you know how this affects shares and the capitalistic image. Gentlemen with big feet might ask why I knew about Moresby and it was a short drive to the Tower, and the Official Secrets Acts are a very sweeping piece of legislation. He was waving it around like toilet paper."

"We have offended," I observed.

"Mightily," Fallon replied. "So I mentioned your name."

"And?"

"Don't ask. The reply was, if that financial hooligan thinks his money and influence can impede the course of justice and national security, he wants to think again, very carefully, about the turbulent world we live in."

"Sounds like a threat."

"And one I should take very seriously. The establishment in this country, Wyatt, plays dirtier than anywhere else. And they're better at it. They've had more practice. I think they're playing for very high stakes."

"Then what?"

"I tugged my forelock, promised to forget I ever asked, and said I'd tell you to do the same."

"Off you go, then."

"Where?"

"Anywhere there are lots of people," Johnny advised. "You've picked up a tail."

Fallon took a stiff pull at the Armagnac. He'd gone slightly grey around the gills.

"Don't panic, Peter," I reassured him. "I think they'll come in to plant a few bugs, see if you're gay or if they can find any dirt on you. We'll wait and tell them you're a raving heterosexual and would like to be seduced by one of their more attractive sisters—about five ten, blond, early twenties, usual dimensions. Off you go."

"You're mad," he insisted.

We waited, Johnny concealed in the kitchen, me in the bedroom. He was carrying, I wasn't, so I selected one of Fallon's neatly rolled umbrellas. Maybe the whole idea was a stupid move, a piece of childish provocation, but maybe it would bring results. I lay on the bed and felt my stomach beginning to turn over, the muscles quivering with anticipation.

They came in through the front door. I hoped they wouldn't check the place out first, but they did, although not very thoroughly. I hid under the bed. Where Johnny concealed himself I don't know, but they didn't spot us. They wired the telephone first, then the area above the front door that catches the conversation when people arrive or leave. Quiet workers both, no unnecessary chatter.

When the bedroom door opened I was lying on the bed and faced with a tall, thin man in a three-piece suit from one of the better multiples. He looked like one of those mid-Atlantic salesmen who carry smart, thin, square briefcases and sell you everything from double glazing to life insurance.

"You're not Françoise, French lessons by appointment." I feigned surprise and eased myself to a standing position.

"Mike," he called, moving toward me as though he meant business.

"Mike can't come," Johnny's voice sounded. "He's too busy looking at the forty-five I've got pointed at him."

I prodded the salesman with the umbrella point.

"Burglars," I whispered. "Back out, very quietly."

He understood my meaning and went to lie on the lounge floor with his mate, a middle-twenties middleweight with a broken, freckled nose. Johnny stood ten feet away, the big .45 Colt auto never wavering.

I frisked the useful-looking character and found a loaded Walther PPK. They had no identification, not even a luncheon voucher between them, and were not talkative. So I tied their thumbs together with string from the kitchen, took their shoes and, to their dismay, their jackets and trousers. They stood, tied back to back, shirt tails covering horrified indignity.

We searched the attaché cases they carried and found assorted surveillance equipment and a camera. We draped the equipment around them, and Johnny played cheese with the flashing Polaroid.

We pinned a photograph to each of them, on the back of which I had written, "There are more photographs of your friends. Your leader may obtain them by telephoning this number after ten tonight—Love, Wyatt."

We called the police, left the door on the latch, and scattered, smartly. Poor Peter Fallon might have some explaining to do. But whoever had sent the plumbers would be the laughingstock of the local nick.

At nine-thirty precisely Sir Nigel Appleton's short, corpulent frame appeared on the TV security screen at the penthouse. We lived in a mad society where we were afraid of our own shadows, locking ourselves behind closed urban doors, needing to identify our visitors—and those are the precautions of the ordinary affluent city dweller. I had to be five times more careful. The security boys were tailing anyone who even mentioned Moresby. Obviously the lid had to be kept on his arrest. I wished someone would let me into the secret.

Appleton took sherry.

"Sorry I was evasive on the phone last night," he apologized. "But I had to take instruction from my client, Sir Philip Moresby."

So someone else knew, and was talking about it.

"How is he?" I demanded.

"Philip is fine, although under arrest for espionage."

"I know."

Appleton did not look surprised. I asked to see Moresby.

"No way. There's a security blanket on all information concerning Philip. I was advised of that when I saw him on Tuesday. Anyway, Philip won't say a great deal because he suspects our conversations are monitored. I wanted to protest but Philip said no. He writes down any instructions and only speaks I believe when he wants his listeners to hear."

Moresby hadn't lost his touch. His back was to the wall, but it wasn't the first time.

"I am to communicate all the information you require. Philip was arrested on Monday at noon and taken to the interrogation centre. He was allowed to call me on Tuesday morning. Of course I went to him immediately and spent the morning with him. I remember hoping we'd be through by lunchtime because that's when I was instructing your solicitor Lewis. And I had a very busy afternoon."

I was ready to tell Appleton to wind up his opening speech when the connection came through. It hit me like the first gloved punch in a boxing bout that wallops you hard on the nose. Your ears ring, your eyes water, and your face feels like it belongs somewhere else.

"You saw Lewis on Tuesday for lunch?" I interrupted.

"Yes, to give him notes on that land transaction."

"Immediately after you saw Moresby?"

"I called in at the office briefly, but yes."

"You're the connection, don't you see? Lewis was killed on Wednesday on his way to see me."

"Are you suggesting what I think you are?" Appleton looked grave, his brain obviously working overtime at the legal implications.

"Everyone who mentions Moresby merits attention from the security services. Fallon's flat was recently entered. Mrs. Burton was warned not to communicate with anyone. I had armed trespassers this morning at Ty Newydd. A man called Llewellyn Jones summons me to the Home Office to-morrow."

"Those are very serious allegations," he warned.

"Facts," I replied.

"Moresby has been interviewed, perfectly properly, by certain high-ranking officers in the security services. They have intimated to him that the Russians wish to exchange him for a British agent they hold."

"Suddenly, Moresby's paymasters surface," I observed.

"And he is found to have a separate bank account in a suburban branch with thirty thousand pounds in it." Appleton looked down at a piece of paper and shook his head.

"I am to give you this document and leave. Remember, Wyatt. We haven't spoken."

So Appleton departed. I had the feeling that maybe he was holding back. Perhaps his duty to his client was in conflict with his patriotism. I didn't know. So I read the letter from Morseby:

My dear Wyatt,

In great haste, Appleton will give you this. Doubtless by now Mrs. Burton has advised you. Please keep her safely somewhere.

Sorry about Lewis. Do not believe terminated with our sanction. Abdul Fahd, People's Bureau used to set me up. I traded low grade for eyes only—own operation—no backup—silly but necessary. 11 A.M. meet observed. Four-man tail. Arrested Monday noon. Centre wants exchange me for S.I.S. agent held—neat. Who wins search me. Possible prosecution. Decision highest level. Trust no one. Do not involve self. Repeat no involvement.

Yours,

P.

I read the letter over and over again. His thoughts were plain but noted. But I had a name—Abdul Fahd. Then I thought about Lewis. They hadn't killed him until he was on his way to see me. That was risky. If they wanted him dead the best time would have been in London. But they'd sent men into open country to do the job.

My thoughts were interrupted by the telephone, the time exactly 10 P.M.

"Mr. Wyatt?" The voice was female, very Roedean and Swiss finishing school.

"Speaking." I pressed the record facility.

"I believe you have some photographs."

"Don't tell me. You're speaking on behalf of *Private Eye*." That got a laugh.

"You have a wicked sense of humour," the girl replied.

"I was born of a satirical age."

"Can we . . ." she paused for a few seconds to let the Wyatt imagination have free run; someone had been checking the files, ". . . meet? Shall we say my flat in half an hour?"

"Shall we say mine?" I countered. "I used to be a doctor so I never make house calls."

"Neutral ground," she suggested. "Then we can decide where to go."

"The Cullinan," I suggested. "In half an hour."

"You have to be a member," she protested. "And I'm not."

"Speak to the manager, Ashley Lavington. Tell him Wyatt sent you, and to look after you."

"Sounds interesting."

"So do you," I replied. "One more thing. Go alone. And don't send anyone round here to turn the place over in my absence. My lads here forgot their Valium pills. Large heavy men make them nervous and positively terrify me. We then have a twitching complaint in the index finger, right hand."

Chapter Fourteen————————

Johnny phoned in. I told him I was going out and where. He had a contact to make and then a date to keep with a cute little brunette, so I told him not to worry about me. I knew he would, but I was a big boy now and could be allowed out. I had a contact number for him so we let it go at that.

Carson was driving the Silver Spirit. He's Fallon's chauffeur, ex-police driver, forty-year-old man mountain who played number eight for the Metropolitan Police. He spotted the tail we'd picked up as we left the penthouse and still had glued to the Rolls when we reached the Cullinan off Berkeley Square.

I stepped out of the Silver Spirit past a commissionaire

wearing grey topcoat and top hat, and made my way through the Regency porch into the Cullinan. No matter how well dressed or well known you are, the Cullinan is strictly a Members Only club. The carpet in the foyer tickles your ankles. There are no kiosks or small desks, only an ornate eighteenth-century rosewood edifice behind which sits a brunette in a long white evening dress. Behind her are two evening-dressed characters of alarming size. They have public school accents and the manners of a gentleman's gentleman.

"Wyatt," I announced.

They knew who I was. I was accompanied by another young lady through to the Cabaret Room where I saw Ashley Lavington entertaining a slim, attractive redhead at a corner table. He saw me and stood up, an ageing sixties swinger with the elegant mannerisms of a professional hotelier. The hair was greying and the lined complexion spoke of the great outdoors.

"Good evening, sir," he greeted me. "Allow me to present Miss Victoria Keane."

I took a slender right arm and kissed the back of the hand lightly. My eyes wandered to the expanse of golden shoulder, the soft curve of the neck, to the golden cleavage of the low-cut white evening dress. The red hair cascaded, the cheekbones were high, the lips lustrous, the complexion slightly freckled. And the eyes were a reddish brown, sparkling like the single diamond on a white choker around her neck. Our eyes met and her look said: So you're Wyatt.

I winked at Ashley, who vanished. A waiter had already brought me a glass and poured champagne from the silver ice bucket on the table.

"How could I keep such a lady waiting?" I smiled.

"I was being very well looked after, Mr. Wyatt. You do things in style."

"I try my best."

She raised her champagne glass. I raised mine and lit her cigarette.

"I came alone," she announced.

"But your guardian angels are sitting outside in a Colt Lancer," I replied. "Watching my guardian angel."

"I didn't know," she confessed. And I believed her.

"Have you dined?" I inquired.

"Well—actually no."

"I expect they can find us a hamburger."

So we dined in the restaurant, as did a cabinet minister, a marquis, and two wealthy film actors. The Cullinan's membership is strictly controlled by Ashley Lavington. He allows no tarts, however expensive, no criminals, none of the unwashed, and no policemen below the rank of commander. The Cullinan possesses two restaurants, a cabaret room, a casino, and in the soundproofed basement a discothèque where the beautiful people go to play.

She enjoyed the Beluga, and then joined me in the entrecôte Bordelaise, which I insist on washing down with Château Lafite. I wanted to talk about her. Which she did, omitting whom she worked for. But I discovered she'd done the little rich girl's tour of Roedean, Swiss finishing school, secretarial college, and a spell as a private secretary for a politician. She stopped at the positive vetting stage. I discovered she lived alone, liked jazz and some rock, had read *War and Peace*, and that her parents lived in Surbiton. She went on skiing holidays and jogged to keep fit. She enjoyed eating out and going to the theatre and cinema.

We were taking coffee and Armagnac. I cracked an occasional joke to make her laugh and she commented again about my sense of humour and my seemingly opulent life style.

"You're not what I imagined," she admitted. "For a start you're not as tall."

"I'm very pleasantly surprised by you," I confessed. "But someone has probably read my file and told you I have two weaknesses."

"And what might those be?" She leaned toward me, in mock conspiratorial fashion.

"A passion for the truth and fishing."

"Not women?" She feigned surprise.

"That's my third," I replied, looking into the flashing brown eyes. "My fourth is a crazy sense of humour. You'll get your pictures back."

"I'd almost forgotten," she admitted. "You entertain me and bring me to exclusive places and I could be falling down on my task."

"Let me be serious, Vicky. I don't know which department you work for, or what your orders are, but I can guess. I don't know what you know but I'll assume nothing. So let me tell you."

I took a risk and spilled out everything I knew. Maybe that was her task, to find out. But somebody somewhere needed to be told you can't sit by and watch your friends in a jam. You can't go around eliminating people who don't fit into your scheme of things. And I told her that.

"When Philip Moresby was younger than me, he put his life on the line in Occupied France many times. And in those days it was for real. Now half the Establishment and maybe some of the security chiefs were sitting on their arses in some safe armchair while the guys like Moresby were doing the dying out there. Come the time he's in trouble, they forget all that. They won't risk a sou off an inflation-proof pension to step out of line and say wait a minute, someone's got it wrong."

"You believe he's innocent. How do you know?" she asked.

"He was sold out once, by an informer. The Gestapo got him. Luckily he got out before the treatment proved fatal. It's against Moresby's religion to go bent. That's the rational and emotional answer. I know where it counts that Sir Philip Moresby is no traitor."

I must have gone over the top about old Philip because she sat and looked into my eyes and said nothing. I didn't know what she was thinking so I apologized.

"Sorry for being serious. Do you gamble?"

"If I had the money," she answered my question automatically, brandy glass hanging from her fingertips. Her mind was on something else.

"Money's not important," I whispered. "People are. Let's go and make the casino profitable."

Well, it turned out the other way. I'm a wizard blackjack player and I took the table for some loose change—about seven hundred—which enabled me to have fun at roulette. Gambling is a mug's game. You don't see starving book-makers or casino operators. There are some guys who win. But they're the professional punters who can afford the bad days that make the good days payday. I don't have a system as such but I know guys who do. By two-thirty I'd won five thousand, and Vicky had turned the grand I'd started her off with into three. She hadn't followed my play all the way. So I changed my chips into money and she handed me hers. I told her to keep it and stop worrying about the morality of taking my stake as well because the parable about the talents usually works out. Unto those who have and invest wisely comes more.

I asked her if she liked discos and she said why not, so we spent the next hour dancing the modern tribal rituals and drinking more champagne. She could hold her alcohol well and I was steady enough. Then we danced close and slow. She was warm and soft and smelled expensive. I wondered whether the golden tan extended all over the slim figure to the toes of what I could see were long legs through a slit at the side of the long white dress. Maybe my pulse rate accelerating was the purpose of our meeting.

We left the Cullinan with a different follower in tow. I had my arm around Vicky and she whispered, "Your flat."

Carson checked the flat out before we went in. There was little chance of a break-in being effected, but I was being cagey. I handed Vicky the photographs as Carson waited outside.

She watched me, the brown eyes playing a game of mental seduction with me. I held her hand.

"Wyatt, do you know what my orders are now?"

I shook my head, poured two Armagnacs, and pressed the button on the stereo. Sounds of Jacques Loussier floated, and I was just a little bit drunk.

"To take you to my flat, give you a nice sleeping tablet. Then two men come in, rough me up a bit, and I scream rape. Cheers." She raised the brandy glass. "Of course, we shoot you full of dope and plant more of the stuff on you, and having pinched your flat keys, plant a load more here."

"Sounds exciting."

"So I've told you; I've blown my cover. You can take your gun off now. I'll do likewise."

She was no fool; I'd put the Walther PPK in my waistband earlier in the evening. I put the gun between the mattress and base of my bed. When I walked into the lounge again she was standing absolutely naked except for a thigh holster at the top of her left leg. A .25 automatic nestled against the inside of her thigh. She threw the holster on top of the rest of her clothes on one of the lounging units.

Then her arms were around me, frisking me in a gentle, playful way. We were kissing long and breathlessly. I was still half expecting a knee in the groin or an aikido hold on one of the pressure points. I hoped it wasn't the one her left hand was moving toward. It's a strange experience trying to make love to a girl and at the same time make sure she's not going to disable you or render you unconscious. She was undressing me, and her flesh was warm and soft and she did have an all-over tan. Then she pulled me toward the bedroom, keeled over on the bed, holding me on top of her. She moved slowly at first, writhing beneath me. She finished with the burst of an Olympic sprinter.

Hours later she was lying on my stomach, giggling occasionally.

"Remind me about the photographs," I whispered.

"That's ironic." She laughed, then spoke softly. "I want you again."

I wondered who was getting the best of this deal. Maybe

she was supposed to destroy my resources. It was eight o'clock and the door buzzer sounded.

"Visitors," I explained.

"Tell them to go away." She pouted.

"Might be your friends."

"You know I came alone." She started sliding down my stomach. I resisted further temptation and extricated myself. I looked round the bedroom door to the screen and saw Johnny standing outside. He had the brunette with him.

"Come ahead," I spoke into the intercom, then went back into the bedroom for a pair of trousers. I was back in the lounge. Johnny looked around at the low lighting, the clothing strewn all over the place. He sniffed the air.

"Perfume. You've got a bird in here."

Felicity said good morning, that she and Johnny had come to cook breakfast, and she took him off to the kitchen. Vicky Keane appeared at the bedroom door wearing a short bathrobe. She collected her clothes and mine too.

"Friends." I walked over and kissed her, then led her back into the bedroom. We sat on the bed. I lit her a cigarette and fetched some brandy. You shouldn't drink it for breakfast.

"You haven't asked me what I know." She put the pictures in her handbag.

"I have three options. One is to throw you out in the street. Very embarrassing trying to hail a taxi when you're beautifully naked. Two is to get Johnny in here and start hurting you. Three is to give you breakfast and have you chauffeured home."

"Left myself open, haven't I?" she admitted. "The first option appeals to your sense of humour. You'd do it. Second option—I think you'd do that. You might still. I don't know how long I'd last, but I'd try damned hard." Her eyes flashed as she spoke.

"You would." I held her hand tight. She squeezed mine.

"It's option three, isn't it, Wyatt?"

I nodded.

"Can I call in?" she asked.

"Be my guest."

The Rolls stopped outside her flat, a basement in the Cromwell Road. Vicky Keane looked at me.

"You haven't asked me what I know."

"When you're ready, you'll tell me."

"Can we drive?"

We drove. I lit her a cigarette, had a thin Havana myself, and coughed. I was smoking too much, drinking too much—well everything too much. I sat back and listened.

She told me about Moresby's arrest, about how the orders came not from M.I.5 but a different department, about how she tailed David Lewis to West Wales and then returned to London. By this time she and a fellow agent called Calladyne had been transferred to a unit commanded by someone called Q. Her next instruction was to contact me and obtain the photographs. She was to try to compromise me and have me hauled off on a rape charge—and that was all she knew.

So I kissed her goodbye, noted a telephone number, and told her to get herself a bigger gun. I told her to be careful, use any information I had given her, and that I'd see her again. Meantime I had a couple of pressing appointments.

Chapter Fifteen————————————

I got back to the penthouse to find Johnny had gone. Fallon was waiting for me, demanding to know who had had his secretary, Felicity. She had been due to meet Fallon and had stood him up. He had called at her flat at breakfast time and she had not been there. I told him he should not mix business with pleasure, and used an external phone. Maybe the phone was bugged; I didn't much care.

I called a number in Tel Aviv and made some noises in a code that must have been years out of date, but I was put through to Isser Bar Lev, an old friend. I needed to locate Fahd and Nury al Said before anyone else did. Who better to ask about evil Arabs than an Israeli?

Bar Lev is a man of few words and no pleasantries. A lonely man, an inconspicuous man, some would say a nondescript man, he knew better than anyone else what went on around the Middle East. He knew more than I did about what was happening in London. He should have. He was head of the Mossad.

I had a twelve o'clock deadline to catch Llewellyn Jones. By the time I had drunk my coffee, the telephone rang. A businesslike voice told me Shalom. If I had a message for the man, be in Hyde Park by eleven.

I just made it. I knew I had a tail. But so did the people I came to meet because my tail disappeared five minutes before a young girl walking an enormous ferocious German Shepherd dog passed me. Thirty yards behind her was a young crew-cut athletic type walking a Doberman. The girl indicated to me to walk with her.

She did not look more than twenty-one, wore a track suit, and possessed the wild, dark, predatory beauty of Israeli youth.

"The man says you need help."

"The man is right," I replied.

"You are an old friend?"

I tried hard to remember the words.

"And getting older."

She smiled. "You are not jogging?"

"I've had too much exercise recently."

"The man says you want Abdul Fahd and Nury al Said. We know them. Fahd is in Tripoli. We are unsure about Said."

"Who is called Q in British Intelligence?"

"Quittenden of S.I.S. They have asked about Said."

"Did they ask about Fahd?"

"No, Fahd was removed from London quickly on Monday. The man says we have no quarrel with Moresby. If we had, we'd kill him."

I believed that very sincerely. Now it was time to chance my arm.

"Can you get me Said and Fahd?"

"Fahd, no. Operation requires political approval. Said—we will find him."

"Who is director of operations, M.I.?"

"Richard Lansbury. He is in London."

She gave me his address. I handed her a card.

"Shalom, Major Wyatt."

"Shalom, Mossad lady."

Llewellyn Jones rose from behind an enormous desk in an oak-panelled office that was elegant, yet claustrophobic. I took an armchair and a very dry sherry and felt tired.

He was about fifty, five nine, and portly. Well, fat really, under the immaculate pinstripes. The face was round, bespectacled, and topped by black, bushy hair. The eyes were steel blue, case-hardened. The gracious manner did not fool me for a moment. Llewellyn Jones might look like a benevolent owl, but when owls start moving, their prey had better look out.

He gave me a few minutes of small talk about the hot weather, how the fish were running at Dysant, and how was the Lord Lieutenant who had been at Cambridge with him. He tried to make me feel like a member of the Establishment. My company was part of the backbone of British industry. Humorous that, because his political masters were pulling it to bits. I was missed at the important functions and city dinners. I gave him full marks for research and waited for the punchline, which came while we were on the lamb cutlets and a second-rate claret at his club. Maybe I'm not Eton and Balliol, but I cannot take to a man who insults you with an inferior wine when you know he knows better.

"Mr. Wyatt. I am in a responsible position at the Home Office."

"I see." I pretended to be thick. But somehow the country bumpkin act was not going to work.

"I was very sorry to hear about your dreadful experience on Wednesday."

"David Lewis wasn't too thrilled."

"Quite so. Very unfortunate. My problem is that Lewis was killed because he was an innocent bystander in a matter the security services are investigating. I am quite unable to elaborate for obvious reasons. I know you are anxious for the people responsible to be apprehended. I want to assure you that they will be. But it is unlikely they will be brought to trial for—reasons of state, shall we say?"

Llewellyn Jones was polite. The message was clear. Wyatt—forget it. Up yours, chum.

"I think I see the problem. But the police have to investigate."

"Mr. Wyatt, I cannot really believe you're that naïve."

Time to drop the country bumpkin act.

"So it's Go Home Wyatt time and forget all about it?"

"I think that would be best." He nodded.

Coffee arrived. He offered me a cigar but I smoked my own. Time to put the boot in.

"Have the security services decided when to charge Sir Philip Moresby?" I enquired.

Llewellyn Jones would be a hard man to play poker against. He did not hesitate for a second.

"I understood he was on holiday. Do you know Philip well?"

"Machiavelli would have been proud of you. I don't think you're some Home Office functionary. I think you are the Home Office, and one or two other places besides. Now I'm sorry to be so blunt and direct after a courteous approach, a good lunch, and mediocre wine. I know about Moresby. I'm not as thick as I look, although I do take some time to catch on. Lewis' death and Moresby's arrest are connected."

"You may be jumping to conclusions," he warned.

"I'll tell you what I think. Moresby was framed. Lewis was killed because he was coming to me. Either the party who set the frame was responsible, or it was your mob trying to keep news of his arrest quiet."

"A very serious allegation. What is your proof?"

I had been fishing in a conjectural way, casting my lure into a deep pool. Maybe the fish had gone. I had waited for the tickle that told me to strike. It had not come. Llewellyn Jones had all the cards and he knew it. So I bluffed.

"My turn to play poker." I smiled.

He looked at me hard for almost a minute, then spoke.

"Some friendly advice Mr. Wyatt. Your little jokes are annoying some of my people. Your egotistical insistence that you have the right to know what is going on is frankly what I would have expected from a man with power and no responsibility. This is not America. The industrial-military complex does not lean on the elected representatives of the people and their servants. We are dealing with a security matter which is the province of government."

"And to hell with David Lewis and Philip Moresby."

"Moresby would be the first man to agree that the security of the state must take priority over the welfare of an individual. You may be an important and powerful man, Mr. Wyatt. But you're not even in the second eleven in this matter."

Then he smiled. "Can I drive you somewhere?"

"Should I accept a ride in your car, or might it be a last journey?"

"Yes, Mr. Wyatt, you certainly have a very dry sense of humour."

I was back in the penthouse doing a lot of hard thinking. Three-fifteen is a bad time to start drinking malt but what the hell—it was a bad time to be Wyatt. I was getting older. Every other enemy I'd been up against had form, substance, defined resources, you knew how he could hurt you and where to hit him. But this wasn't soldiering—I didn't know what it was. Llewellyn Jones had worried me. They had me on the run. I did not know what to expect or where to expect it from.

The world is a big place, but if someone wants you badly enough and will devote time and money to it, there is no place to hide. My options were easy. Duck out and live happily ever after. Or stay and take whatever consequences came, with no guarantee of success.

Johnny returned at four. I did not give him the chance to say anything but told him what I was thinking. He poured some tonic water, kicked one of the lounging units out of the way, and sat down on the floor.

"I'm not the guy to ask. I quit the old country back in fifty-six. You can't fight tanks with stones, so we got the shit kicked out of us. There was nowhere to hide. It was run or die. I ran."

"You went to see what you could do in Czechoslovakia in sixty-eight. And you keep in touch with resistance."

"Sure. If I thought there was a cat in hell's chance I might have gone to Poland in eighty-one—might. But for what? You can't beat the system. Someone always tries, someone always will. And in my country someone's got to, because the damn system is wrong. The state wants to control what you think. There is only one way—the Party's way.

I poured myself another malt.

"Llewellyn Jones seems to think it's not our affair. I suppose he is right. Of course he is right—from his point of view, and he can back his point of view up."

"Say Moresby is a traitor. Would you leave him?"

"He is a friend," I replied.

"And say he killed Lewis?"

"I'd want to know why. Then I'd turn him in."

"Wyatt, you got one hell of a strange way of doing things."

"Are you with me?"

"As long as it takes. Now pay attention. There is movement out on the streets."

I found Richard Lansbury propping up the bar of an afternoon drinking club in Soho. Not the sort of place you'd expect to find him. But he used to be a cop. Coppers and villains are mostly the same type of people with different viewpoints. Lansbury had gone to the club for his own reasons.

We gained entry by offering the doorman five quid. The anthropoid shuffled out from his hole, looked us up and down, eyeing Johnny suspiciously.

"You're not looking to give Mac trouble are you?" he grunted.

"No," I replied wearily. "We are but tired thirsty travellers along life's hard road."

The goon had heard the words but did not understand. Maybe his vocabulary did not stretch that far. He shuffled back to his hole and we were in a small smoky cellar with the clunk of fruit machines, shrill noises of electronic games, and the smell of stale beer.

A couple of passable tarts looked up from their drinks as we moved to the bar. A gaggle of retired recidivists were playing crib in a corner. Four untidy youngsters were flicking cigarette ash aimlessly as they talked in low voices. The minder was playing Space Invaders. He looked across, saw Johnny, and went back to playing Space Invaders.

The barman was a small, chirpy individual wearing a loud waistcoat and matching bow tie.

"Afternoon, gents," he greeted us breezily. It was too much.

"Whisky and a tonic water. In separate glasses. And whatever he's having."

I indicated the corner of the bar where Lansbury sat. He had the same sulky spaniel look I remembered, but the lines were deeper. He crushed his cigarette into the ashtray and lifted his beer glass.

"Cheers," he said wearily.

I moved toward him. Johnny went to the end of the bar and sat, back to the wall, watching.

"Big boy," Lansbury observed. "So what brings you into my life, Wyatt, after an absence of so many years? Don't tell me. You want some information."

"I thought a chat."

"Not safe to be seen talking to you."

"So who's looking?"

He did not answer, but gazed into his beer for a moment as though seeking inspiration.

"You really are flavour of the month in our circles. What is your motive? Get someone out, right or wrong?"

"Get someone out—right. Wrong—leave him where he is but let me have answers."

"Thought so. It's out of my hands. I don't know what's going on. Take my advice and leave it that way."

"Last word?"

"Except how did you find me?"

"With difficulty."

"Thanks for the drink. And Wyatt—"

"Yes?"

"You can get buried in this game."

Chapter Sixteen

I stood in the small churchyard on a windswept hill at ten fifty-five on Saturday, August 28. I turned the collar of my black overcoat up against the biting northeasterly wind. The sky was a mass of billowing grey.

The funeral cortège wound its way slowly up the long hill. Six grim-faced men carried the polished casket that took David Lewis on his last journey. A solemn, shuffling mass of mourners, feet scrunching on the gravel, followed Ann Lewis and her daughter, who walked slowly behind the coffin. They were accompanied by a middle-aged man whose eyes met mine for a moment.

Ann Lewis wore black, was hauntingly, fearfully striking beneath the veil, dark pools of eyes swirling with sorrow. The daughter, almost a woman, tall as her mother, held her arms, eyes misted over with tears, her young face grey with grief. She drew level with me, watching me all the time. She stopped. I said nothing because I did not know what to say. She did.

"You killed my father."

Now I've been scared witless a few times when the air has been hissing death and we've been up against it. But I'd never been so alone as I was hearing those words. The chill cut me in places I couldn't feel. The girl's expression was neither hostile nor hysterical. Her mother stopped, looked at me. I looked back and could say nothing. The cortège moved on. A hundred pairs of eyes regarded me as the lowest form of life.

I stood alone as the church door shut. I did not have the

courage to walk in. As an excuse I kept telling myself I should leave the grief to Lewis' family and friends. I had been no friend to him, even in never knowing him. I'm not a religious person. But all I could hear were the girl's words, spoken simply and without malice: "You killed my father."

Maybe this was the apotheosis of all the enemies I'd ever killed coming at me in one blindingly simple sentence. You killed my father. My hands were shaking. I thrust them deep in my coat pockets and stood alone on that hill, condemned to the silence of the tombstones and the indifference of the grey skies, while inside the church everyone paid their last respects.

I heard the crunch of footsteps on the gravel not five yards away. I half turned and saw Detective Chief Superintendent Dan Caswell. He stood, hatless, a black coat collar turned up against the wind, foxy features expressionless.

"Going in?" he asked.

"Haven't got the guts."

"I've been watching from over there. Sort of feeling the same way myself."

I respected him for what I thought was a lie.

"We have to face it sometime." He paused for a few seconds. "Besides, it's bloody cold out here."

The door creaked noisily as Caswell opened it. Most of the congregation looked round. The service was in progress and I'd intruded again. We found a pew at the back. I was looking in from the outside. Everything had a distant, unreal quality about it. Caswell sang the hymns in lusty fashion, intoned the prayers, nodded at the clergyman's eulogy. I lost track of time.

I remember standing outside in the cold again as the mourners filed away from the graveyard. Caswell and I were alone, the only sound the sexton's spade shovelling earth into the grave. We stood saying nothing. After a while we walked away and I realized we had both stood at attention for the customary silence.

Involuntarily I had paid my last respects.

"Can you give me a lift into Pontowyn?" he asked. "I came up with the local patrol car."

He nodded appreciatively as we climbed into the black Silver Shadow. As we approached a local pub he cleared his throat.

"Dry," he said. "Could you use one?"

The lounge bar was deserted. Caswell ordered two whiskies and we sat in a corner. He coughed over one of my thin Havanas.

"Bad business all round," he muttered.

"Any sign of Said?"

He shook his head. "But I have news. My chief won't press for charges against you for killing Bannion."

"Should hope not," I replied.

"If you drop the armed trespass charge against those two men."

"Naughty."

"If you decline, I never offered the deal."

"I accept."

"What are you up to?" he asked, casting me one of his sly looks.

"I've been warned off at a very high level."

"I see."

"And you?" I asked.

"Can't discuss police business."

I bought some more drinks. He was watching me, smiling to himself.

"Don't trust me, do you, Wyatt?"

"I trust everybody," I replied. "I've been very open to all I've met."

"What will you do?" he asked. "Forget it?"

"Can't."

"Me neither. I've handled twenty-six murder investigations for twenty-six convictions. But I can't see myself getting this one."

"Pity to spoil a winning streak. Got any room to manoeuvre?"

"No jerk from the big city tells me how to run my patch, especially if he hasn't the guts to do it to my face. My chief told me to drop it after orders from on high. But I've put the alert out for Said with Interpol. This morning the chief was checking my manpower disposition. He advised me to take the guard off Mrs. Lewis."

Alarm bells started ringing. I still had her covered, but that cover was down to one man.

"Did you?"

He shook his head. "I'm not very good at taking orders, especially when they're wrong. So at my next interview with the chief, I hand in my badge if I'm ordered to stop covering the Lewises."

"I expect Aberinvest needs a good security consultant."

"That sounded like a charitable bribe." He looked angry. "I can look out for myself."

"Deal, Caswell?"

"Let's hear it."

"I've got men looking for Said—don't look so worried, they're not contract killers. After I've finished with him, you can have him, then make your case. In the meantime, keep me posted."

"What happens if I repeat this conversation?" he asked.

"Go ahead. I'll still get to Said."

"Deal, Wyatt. But I want him alive."

"I won't kill him," I promised.

Ty Newydd was secure and quiet. I had a late lunch and retired to my study for a short nap. Sam woke me at four wondering whose hands I'd got into in London because she'd been tidying my clothes and found lipstick on a shirt collar and red hair on my jacket.

I needed some answers from Mrs. Burton. We covered her story step by step. Richard Lansbury had been with a certain Calladyne and a girl I took to be the delicious Vicky Keane when they arrested Moresby. I was trying to piece together who was involved and who had done what. A gem of an idea had occurred to me. Quittenden was number three in S.I.S. and I kept asking myself why they were involved. Counterespionage was M.I.5's job. We reasoned Quittenden's involvement as a political decision. He sounded as if he'd go well with Llewellyn Jones, who seemed to be some kind of Prime Ministerial éminence gris.

We were moving in the highest circles.

The Israeli Embassy telexed at 6:03 P.M. using an old book code. The old book proved to be the Koran. You've got to hand it to them, when the chips are down they're safer than Rothschilds. Sam played with the computer which translated for me:

CONFIRM LOCATION FAHD. CONFIRM POLITICAL SANCTION FOR SNATCH DENIED. OBSERVATION MAINTAINED. LOCATION SAID BEST BET SWITZERLAND. INVESTIGATION CONTINUING. INTERCEPT COMPANY SIGNAL TO CIRCUS 2000 MONDAY. NO INVOLVEMENT WITH MONITOR. INTERCEPT CENTRE SIGNAL TO MARGARET 1400 TODAY. CONCLUDE NIMROD SOONEST.

The second part meant nothing to me. Mrs. Burton supplied the explanations.

"Intercept Company signal to Circus—C.I.A. to S.I.S. Monitor is Moresby. They're denying involvement. It appears the Americans have nothing to do with Sir Philip's arrest. Centre to Margaret—that's K.G.B. Lubyanka H.Q. to London Embassy. Conclude Nimrod soonest—whatever that means. Nimrod was a hunter. Can't help there. Wait a moment, there is more."

COMPUTER BEST BET HOSTILE ACTION V. MONITOR. CENTRE. REPEAT CENTRE.

"Interesting," Mrs. Burton thought aloud. "It appears that the Mossad won't tell us how, but they believe the K.G.B. is the organization that framed Sir Philip."

The problem with spooks is you never know which one to trust. Deceit is their stock in trade. Each action seems to be capable of many interpretations. You never know who the good guys and the bad guys are. If you solve that problem, just to confuse you, they each act like the other should.

If Moscow Centre was involved, how the hell did we prove it?

Meanwhile Caswell had arrived. Five minutes later he was in my study with a scotch.

"Nice little cottage, this," he observed. "I've been instructed to remove the guard on Mrs. Lewis, eight P.M. deadline."

I glanced at the clock. Seven-fifteen.

I can stretch it to eight-thirty. Any later and I join the dole queue."

"Anyone else in the house except the Lewises?"

"Arthur and Megan Roberts were still there half an hour ago, but not planning to stay the night. I'll go back and relieve my lads. Down to you, then. Do you know where the house is?"

"Yes. I'll meet you in that wooded area by the roadside, four hundred metres up from the house."

"Silly question." Caswell grinned. "I suppose you've had the house watched?" he joked.

"Of course."

"My lads have never seen anyone. Are you serious?"

"Exactly what you'd expect to see why my boys are on recce."

"I was right about you, Wyatt. You don't trust anybody."

I left word for Johnny to follow us up. If he hadn't arrived by eleven, Bill Grant was to come in his place. That left two to guard Ty Newydd, and, counting me, three on the ground. Ty Newydd's defences were a bit thin if this was a feint to draw us off, but a risk is a risk.

I was in the wooded area near the Lewis house by eight-thirty. I parked the old Land Rover next to Caswell's car. To avoid suspicion, I'd taken the Land Rover, which could belong to any old farmer out on an agricultural chore, even late on a Saturday night—provided no one saw me.

I was head to toe in camouflage gear, S.A.S. balaclava, the lot. The Rolls-Royce of handguns, a Smith and Wesson .357 Magnum was holstered on my right side. Bowie knife, original design, eleven and a half inches, razor-sharp cutting edge and top ellipse, was tied down to my left thigh. Main armament was a ten-bore Magnum gas-operated shotgun, made specially by an American company. The barrel was illegal according to the Firearms Act, being only twenty inches long. But at thirty yards, it chucked out almost as much lead as a sub-machine gun in a nice even pattern. I had twenty spare rounds for the shotgun, plus five in the magazine, and thirty for the .357 plus six in it. To be safe you should keep five in a revolver, hammer resting on an empty chamber. But when you're looking for trouble, load all six.

Caswell sat behind a hedge and looked down a sloping field to the Lewis house, two hundred yards away. He didn't hear me approach.

"Jesus!" he exclaimed, as I tapped his shoulder. "Don't do that. You just took ten years off my life. Have you got a licence for all that?" He looked at the weaponry I carried.

"Most of it." I indicated to move to the small wood across the field. From there I could see the driveway and the field behind the house. My blind spot was the other end of the house. No one could come that way unnoticed because a ten-acre field sloped toward the house, and I had a very good view of that field and three of its hedgerows. The gate was at the top, and the roadside hedge so thick that no one would get in that way—quietly. I shifted my night glasses to the ground and handed Caswell the coffee flask. Then I gave the magpie call and was answered by a jay from outside the wood to our right.

"What's all that about?" Caswell asked, voice low. He

122

reached for his cigarettes but I put my hand on the packet of Capstan.

"No smoking," I ordered. "Smell it half a mile off in this weather."

I didn't hear Ko until he was ten yards from us. Caswell didn't hear him until Ko knelt beside him. Heckler-Koch ready, bow and arrows slung over his back.

"Iesu Mawr." Caswell put his hand out to me. "Wyatt, I'm glad I've got a strong heart."

"This is the jay," I replied.

"Police gone," Ko reported. "No one about. Farmer gone home." He indicated a farmhouse half a mile away.

I looked down at the house, standing in half an acre of garden, screened from the roadway by conifers. The garden was mostly lawn, dotted with shrubs. The driveway was tarmac and the paths concrete. No loose chippings to warn us of intruders or to worry about if we had to go in close. Hedges surrounded three sides of the garden, but a post and rail fence cordoned off the back garden. From our elevation we could see well enough to ensure that no one crossed the ground without being spotted. A car stood in the driveway— Arthur Roberts' car, according to Caswell.

Dusk is the best time of day, next to dawn. Birds fly in to roost and the still air becomes alive with their sound. Sun disappears to a dying westward pale glow, shadows descend. But movement on the ground and in the air plays tricks with your eyes. Sounds carry better, air becomes crisper, your sense of smell more acute. Caswell left us at ten, then Arthur Roberts and wife drove off.

At eleven it was very quiet. I felt foolish about being in that wood dressed as a border raider. Then Ko touched my arm, signalled movement, then held two fingers out. It was dark now; there were lights on in the house, but no one had drawn any curtains. There was a new moon, not much cloud, and I could see fifty yards. I knew Ko could see at least a hundred.

He'd spotted two men moving. They must have left a vehicle a long way off because nothing had come down or up the road for the last half hour. But that was as far as their experience went. They were walking, whispering to each other. So we moved back into some bushes.

I could see them. They came to the edge of the wood, almost where we'd been positioned, and stood. One carried a rucksack on his back and wore hiking gear. I could see long hair and a solid frame. The other was smaller, also dressed in hiking gear. The first man unshipped his rucksack, and took out a case. There were sounds of metal meeting metal. Both men were now crouching down, five yards from us. I could see the shape of a scoped rifle being rested against the hedge.

"We wait," whispered the heavy man. "Orders are get both of them."

They did not sound like the home-grown variety of nasty, more like imported talent.

"Leave it an hour," the second replied. "We can break in, do the job at close quarters. Two women—what's the problem?"

The first man chuckled. The second cut in.

"What you're thinking about is against orders." Then he started laughing. "But who's to know?"

Their conversation had taken a very unpleasant turn and I got angry. For two pins I'd have cut the bastards down where they skulked, but I could see two walking pieces of information in front of us. I tapped Ko, signalled I'd take the big one, and to leave them alive. My pulse rate upped and my stomach tightened, and in we went.

My man turned to see the toe of the shotgun catch him under the chin; his head snapped back into unconscious oblivion. Ko was already on his man, knife at his throat before I'd taken my man out.

"Quiet or die," Ko whispered, his flat broad face next to his victim's.

I tied the man's hands behind him, thumbs with string trick, whipped his belt from him and strapped his legs up. I did the same for his mate, who was out cold. Ko shoved his man to sit at the base of a tree while I grabbed the armament. One Makarov 7.65-mm automatic, one razor, one short switchblade, and a neat little assemble-yourself, high-velocity .223 four-shot sniper's rifle, maker unknown.

"Who are you?" the captive whispered, terrified eyes on the point of Ko's knife that pressed against his throat.

"Tuan ask questions." Ko smiled.

"Up yours," the captive replied. He had a transatlantic accent but he was German, and had learned American, not English. He was young, no more than thirty, with neutral features.

Neither man had documentation. This was getting to be standard. But they were not trained agents. The way they'd moved and their conversation spelled criminal to me. The equipment in the haversack confirmed it. Infiltrators would have carried more sophisticated gear.

"I haven't got all night," I explained to the German. "And neither have you. I want to know your life history and who sent you for what, down at that house. Ko will kill you unless you cooperate. First he'll cut off your ears, then think what other parts don't have any bones in the way."

I nodded to Ko, and took three steps away after stuffing an oily rag in the German's mouth. We didn't want any screams to wake distant neighbours. Now, I've never tortured a prisoner in my life, and I stopped Ko from that practise the first day I met him. But I've never been averse to bluffing even to the extent of chucking a dead terrorist from a chopper to make his mate think I threw uncooperative live ones out. It always worked, maybe because I was a convincing actor. Some of the guys I've known have made a habit of torture, but never while I've commanded them. Start getting your jollies that way and it's time you worked for subhuman butchers who give you all that crap about it being part of their religious beliefs that prisoners are dishonoured and no longer worth consideration.

The German started screaming through the gag, and I let him think for ten seconds that Ko was about to amputate his left ear. He deserved a scare for thinking evil thoughts about playing with Mrs. Lewis and her daughter.

"Listening time." I pulled the gag out and Ko smiled. It's not Ko's fault he's a slab-faced Mongoloid who looks like a horror film extra with a grin that would frighten a vampire.

These two had been hired Friday night by a London firm of criminals to kill both Lewises and, if possible, make it look like suicide. He was well-briefed with photographs, locations, and plans of the house, and had been promised a clear run by a man named Souter who had done the deal and paid him five thousand up front with a further five to come. The rest of his conversation did not have any relevance to the situation, but would be interesting to a policeman. I knew of a policeman I owed a favour to.

And we had another name—Souter.

Chapter Seventeen————

Ko put the German named Schmidt to sleep with a sword-edged blow. He gagged both of the men and left them in a pile in the bushes. Something was very wrong. Cops called off and then killers sent to the Lewises. Too convenient for a coincidence.

Johnny arrived just after twelve. An hour later I was thinking it was now all a waste of time when the unexpected happened. A car drove slowly down the road from Pontowyn, showing only sidelights. A second car followed, again with only sidelights. The first car stopped in the gateway of the Lewis drive. I used the nightglasses and saw a middleweight

126

hardnose wearing an anorak and carrying what looked like a transmitter-receiver handset. He moved into the hedge by the gateway, out of sight of the road. Both cars continued to the house; the second, a large Volvo estate, reversed up to the front door.

I sent Ko to take out the sentry, gently. The house was in darkness. If the cars' occupants were up to no good, they were being very casual about it. A man got out of the Volvo and a woman from the first car, a Metro. I'd never seen the man before, but the woman was the delicious Vicky Keane.

Johnny had his Kockler sighted on the pair of them. Clear images through his night sight at two hundred yards gave him two kills any time he squeezed off. Johnny is that good.

The man rang the doorbell. Lights went on in the house. I wondered what the hell was going on as the man put his hand in his coat pocket and withdrew it, slowly, empty of any weapon. He held out the hand as Ann Lewis answered the door. He seemed to be showing her some kind of identification. She let them in and Johnny lowered the rifle.

"Bad moment there," he whispered. "Whatever they want doesn't look dangerous, yet."

"You work the back, I'll take the front."

We moved our separate ways. I was fifty yards from the gate when I heard Ko's nightjar call. He'd got the sentry. I moved toward the house down one hedgerow. The front door was shut, but I could hear voices coming from a downstairs room at the end of the house on the left. There was a fanlight window open; the curtains were drawn. I worked round the end of the house and Johnny was at the back, waiting next to some French windows. I signalled and he passed me a celluloid strip. I would enter by the front door. He would use the French windows.

It took me a minute before the catch fell back with a noise I thought should have woken the dead. Nobody heard. I found myself in a large hallway, staircase leading off to the left, three doors to the right. Near the stairs was a dog basket.

Now where was the bloody dog? Judging by the size of its basket, it wasn't a large dog, and therefore the worst kind. They yap and sink teeth into your ankles. I tried to hear the conversation going on in the room while listening for the dog.

"Mrs. Lewis. You have to come with us. It is a matter of security." Vicky Keane's voice.

"I want to telephone someone first. I can."

"I'd rather you didn't." Vicky Keane again.

"Leave that phone alone." Ann Lewis' voice this time. I heard movement, then a man's voice, a cold insistent voice that meant what it said.

"You like your dog, Mrs. Lewis? Just do as you're told—"

Then the dog howled. Somebody screamed. Why did he have to be cruel to animals?

I went in fast, the Magnum ready for use.

Inside, Ann Lewis and her daughter had rushed forward to protect the dog, a terrier-like mongrel. A razor-cut blond character held it by the scruff of its neck. The women were in my line of fire. Everyone looked at me. The Lewis girl screamed at what must have been a frightening sight—a masked armed man. The blond guy, a useful-looking character of medium height and weight, moved fast, dropping the dog and seizing the Lewis girl to use as a shield. She was screaming in pain at the pressure on her left arm.

"Drop your gun," he growled at me. "Or I break her neck."

Ann Lewis, horrified, looked at me. Vicky Keane smiled.

"Do as he says, Mr. Wyatt."

Then she did a very careless or deliberate thing. She ignored Johnny, who had entered in the confusion, and walked toward me. The rule is for a trained person, don't get in lines of sight or fire. Johnny hit the blond guy with the butt of his Kockler. The Lewis women had picked up the dog and were huddled together. The blond guy was on the Axminster. Vicky Keane stood in front of me and winked.

"You got my message, then."

"What message?" I removed my balaclava. "Take the sofa, darling."

What was going on?

"Sorry for the intrusion." I turned to Ann Lewis, elegant in a long kimono, beautiful and devoid of makeup.

"Let's go get some coffee." I took her by the arm and led her toward the door, then turned to the daughter. "We haven't been introduced, young lady."

"Siân," Ann Lewis replied. The girl regarded me suspiciously. Ann Lewis took me into the kitchen. I lit her cigarette. Her slender hands trembled, the eyes watching me uncertainly.

"What happened?" I asked.

"Why are you here?" she demanded.

"To protect you," I replied. "Now what happened?"

She was confused, didn't know who to trust. She was halfway through the cigarette already.

"They came, showed me identification, said they were from security. They wanted Siân and me to pack and move to a safe house, I think they said. The girl did all the talking, said David was killed because he came to see you, that he was carrying a message for a spy they'd caught. I don't believe it, not David. When I wanted to phone, they said no; the man grabbed Skipper—and then you came. I don't know what's happening. I don't know who you really are, or why—"

"Drink your coffee. I don't know what's happening yet. But I'm making progress."

Then I watched the girl who was watching me, scared maybe, but defiant. I didn't have time to muck about. I took the Magnum from its holster, handed it to the girl. She looked at it, scared yet understanding, then took the butt from my grasp and almost dropped the gun on the floor.

"If you believe I had any part in killing your father, or that I mean you any harm, use that gun. If you can't, your mother can."

Both women looked at each other for a moment. The girl

held the gun by her side. Then she raised it, and I thought my gamble hadn't paid off. I didn't think she'd hit me, even at fifteen feet. But that wasn't the point.

"Take it, please," she cried, tears in her eyes, I did, then she fell against me, weeping. Her mother looked on, a strange look in her eyes I couldn't read.

"I think, Mrs. Lewis, you ought to go and pack some clothes, then stay with me for a few days—don't look so alarmed, not at Dysant, at Ty Newydd. We've got a few friends staying as well, so you'll have company."

"Do we have a choice?" Ann Lewis asked.

"Certainly, you can stay here. But it just means my scouts have to camp out in the woods at night, and they're not used to living rough these days. I think they've done enough of that."

"You mean you've been having us watched?"

"Yes. Just in case something like tonight happened."

Johnny took the Lewises to Ty Newydd. Ko bundled the unconscious sentry and blond heavy into the Volvo, then tipped the Kraut and his friend in their car, which he found up the road. I called Caswell from the Lewis house, told him what he'd find but to leave me out of it. That left me with Vicky Keane, watching the moonlight at 3:23 A.M. Expensive perfume floated on the night air. She held my hand and I lit her a cigarette.

"So you didn't get my call?" she asked. "Explains the very offhand way you treated me in there. You thought I was stitching you up, as they say."

"Until you moved into my line of fire. What gives?"

"I called your home, spoke to a girl called Sam who says she's your secretary. This was about eleven thirty-five. I told Calladyne I was ringing a boyfriend. I told her Mrs. Lewis could be in trouble and to tell you. Who is Sam?"

"My secretary."

"Do you sleep with her?"

"Sometimes. What else?"

"Q ordered us down to take the Lewises to a safe house on the Gower. All I know. Lots of orders, no reasons. He didn't expect we'd have any trouble. Calladyne'll be awake soon—this'll look fishy."

"I'll make it look good."

"Wyatt, I don't go to bed with just anyone, not even under orders. You're becoming special for me. Watch your step. Q thinks you're tied in with Moresby and you're bent. You're an all-round embarrassment."

"Spent thirty-five years practising. Success is its own reward," I quipped.

"If Moresby is innocent and whoever framed him knows about you, you haven't got a friend in the world. All sides'll be after you."

"At least I know who my enemies are. Free-fire zones all around."

"Damn you. Be serious."

She put her arms around my neck and kissed me, and I knew she was. We kissed for a few seconds and I extricated myself.

"Being too close to you gives me ideas."

"Me too," she whispered. "I'll let you know what happens."

"Vicky. Be very careful."

Dawn at Ty Newydd is a sight to inspire the poets and awe the gods. Sunrise was a brilliant shade of purple turning through deep red into bright orange against the high, wispy cirrus. The dawn air was clear, clean, and promising. I walked the grounds, past the stables and twenty acres of paddocks, over Home Farm to the head of the valley. The view swept down two miles to the sea. The sun rising higher dappled reflections over the deep blue of the Irish sea, and a heat haze hovered below the horizon.

Wood-pigeons were flying away to the corn from the wooded valley slopes, wings whistling in the still morning air.

131

A crow called noisily and dozens of woodland birds chattered a welcome to the new day. I found a convenient log and sat. A rabbit, blissfully unaware of human intrusion, nibbled away at young grass on the edge of the field just above the wood. A scampering sound on my left showed me another rabbit only feet away. A cock blackbird saw my arm movement and rattled his warning call to the surrounding bushes.

Maybe that was all I had achieved so far: clumsily warning everyone that I was interested. I sat and thought for a while and pondered Mr. Souter's involvement. Was he another link in a chain that led nowhere? I thought about Vicky Keane. She'd turned out to be quite a girl. I trusted her as much as any other player in the game and more than most, but I had reservations. I hoped her professional training would take care of her because we were up against power and resources and probably people who could run rings around me.

I hoped a stay at Ty Newydd would ease the pain for the Lewises and keep my conscience at rest. I was scared about how this whole business might end. Then I walked back to the house and told myself to go to bed, alone, and try to sleep.

Johnny had his contacts acquiring information about Mr. Souter. And I had a plan for a little conversation with this broker of contract killings.

Chapter Eighteen

Isser Bar Lev, taciturn head of Israel's legendary secret service, received the signal at 9:15 A.M. on Sunday, August 29. He had not slept for two days because two of his specialist teams were scotching a P.L.O. operation to raid the Israeli Embassy in Paris. Monday's *Le Monde* would record the murders of two Arabs gunned down as they left an apartment in the Latin Quarter. It would not reveal the Mossad's involvement with the French Action Service in raiding four further apartments, a garage, and the taking of Futrelle, France's most wanted gangster.

Bar Lev read the signal from Zurich. Nury al Said was hiding in Lugano at a small pension. Turning to his aide, Bar Lev spoke quietly:

"Grab him. Air freight to London tonight."

The aide nodded. Bar Lev handed a piece of paper to the communications officer.

"Signal London. I'll be at home, but only if it's urgent."

At 2:46 P.M. a Mercedes transit van pulled up at the front of the Pension du Lac in Lugano. Seconds later, Nury al Said was assisted, staggering, down the steps, supported by a young woman and a tall man, who helped him into the back of the van. Passersby hearing the conversation concluded the dark-skinned young man was drunk. The transit was driven at a leisurely pace across the St. Gotthard, through mountain tunnels to Lucerne and on to Zurich.

At an eighteenth-century house in a residential district, Said was swathed in bandages and sedated. An ambulance took him to the airport. Customs clearance was swift. The stretcher was placed aboard an El Al flight to London. By 9:30 P.M. he was locked in the basement of a small country house on the outskirts of Swindon.

In Lugano at 10:03 P.M. an attractive girl wearing jeans and a striped T-shirt asked the proprietor of the Pension du Lac for Pierre Auguste, Said's registered alias. An irate proprietor informed this well-spoken French demoiselle that Auguste had departed that afternoon with some drunken friends after a noisy drinking party in his room. There had been complaints and he had not seen Auguste since, nor did he want to. The girl was told she could not see Auguste's room. But the pension proprietor was Italian and subject to two blandishments the girl offered: a hint of sex and the exchange of cash for the key. The girl entered the room, found a rucksack containing clothes, Swiss currency hidden in its lining, and a half-empty bottle of gin. Empty wine bottles littered the room. Three used glasses stood on a table. By the time the proprietor went up to collect on the first proposition the girl had disappeared. She had left via the fire escape.

At 11:05 P.M. in the Russian Embassy annex an irate Vladimir Baikal verbally abused his colleague in Zurich for business incompetence. Baikal's fear of being moved to Siberia as commissioner for Internal Security was the real motive for his lack of patience with the Zurich office. Baikal was grateful that Alexei Svetkin had already retired for the night. He hoped vainly that by the time Svetkin awoke the Zurich office might know the whereabouts of Nury al Said. He did not sleep well, but pondered the identity of Said's drinking partners. Had British Intelligence beaten his men to the objective?

Ten minutes later, a forty-year-old man picked up a Sunday newspaper and read a confession by a man given to understand that there would be no prosecution for sins committed against security in 1958. He smiled to himself and thought of Sir Philip Moresby.

"How are the mighty fallen," he spoke aloud. "Alpha is the key."

The man no longer smiled. He was known only as Alpha.

Across in Lancaster Gate, Simon Quittenden switched his office light off and walked to the building's entrance. A silent guard watched him walk out onto the street. Quittenden was going home for the first time for a week.

As he walked, he reflected on the week's events. He had the position he wanted: Moresby's job. He had gathered evidence, he had waited, watched, investigated. His agents had been made fools of on two occasions by a man called Wyatt. But Moresby was still securely held. The Russians had made more noises about an exchange of agents. But Quittenden needed one more move before Moresby could be prosecuted or exchanged. Tomorrow he would arrange that move.

*****

Sir Philip Moresby put aside *War and Peace* at 11:55 P.M. and got up from the armchair. He poured himself another port and lit his Havana cigar. Quittenden had ensured that Moresby, although a prisoner, received the best treatment.

They pestered him from time to time with visits. Lansbury had been. Down to earth, no-nonsense Richard Lansbury, with his twenty-year-old briar pipe and the same appalling mixture of tobacco that reminded Moresby of the many occasions they had worked together.

He knew the conversations were all monitored. The danger in relaxed, informal reminiscences was that something might slip out. A word out of place, an anecdote that did not fit, and it would all be over. Forty years work would vanish overnight. Quittenden would go through the transcripts, feed the words into his computer systems, and analyse the results. And Moresby was nearer the fatal accident he feared would happen too soon.

That afternoon Quittenden had called again. They had talked, about the weather, the economy, and about *War and Peace*. Quittenden knew something of Tolstoy but not about Dostoevsky. After half an hour he had introduced a girl, the same girl who had been in his office the day he was arrested, then Quittenden departed, leaving them alone.

She was an attractive girl, long red hair, he guessed in her early twenties. She reminded him of someone he had known forty years ago in France. She had the same gazellelike quality, the aristocratic beauty, the style in clothes, although Moresby's someone would never have worn a skirt that split to the thigh, and in those days all women wore brassières.

He watched her brown eyes as she talked about loyalty, about principles, about betrayal. Quittenden had put her up to it, of course. It was deliberate, because the someone this girl, Victoria Keane, reminded him of had also been quite a lady. A French countess, Elise. Moresby had met her in the S.O.E. days in 1943, in Occupied France.

He had fallen in love with her. A young British officer who led

Maquisards against the Wehrmacht loved the wife of a member of the Laval government, a collaborateuse. It had been the best cover in the world, for Elise was the best double agent he had known. She provided top-class information, and on several occasions participated in raids against the sale Boche. She was an aristocrat in her own right, but a member of the Communist Party, and the only woman he had ever really loved.

They had spent time together, stolen hours, talking, discussing the world after the defeat they were sure would be inflicted on the Germans, laughing, and making love. When the Gestapo net closed on the Maquisards, Elise had sent the warning that saved his life and left her in the hands of subhuman torturers. It was said her husband had watched as, for three days, an S.S. colonel had inflicted unspeakable horrors on Elise. But she died before breaking.

The night after the Normandy landings, Moresby had gone personally to the château with four men. Crazy with grief, heart full of revenge, he had shot M. le Comte four times in the stomach and once under each kneecap. Elise's husband had taken three days to die a painful death.

Three days later, Moresby ambushed the S.S. colonel's car, killed the driver and four escorts, and hung the colonel upside down from a tree. Then he had cut the man's throat.

Now Elise's ghost sat opposite him. The memories overwhelmed him, but he sat silently, listening. Quittenden was determined to destroy him. And there was no Elise to warn him, no way to fight off the memories.

He answered some of Victoria Keane's questions, which she put conversationally, informally. He used them to evaluate what Quittenden knew.

"And you know Mr. Wyatt," she stated. Not a question, but a statement.

"Yes."

"He's a friend?"

"A very good friend," Moresby replied, knowing the direction in which the conversation was heading.

"You'd like him too, Miss Keane. Sort of young fellow that appreciates the company of beautiful women."

"I had dinner with him the other evening."

"You see what I mean."

Vicky Keane remembered Richard Lansbury's advice to her the afternoon Moresby was arrested. She could understand why Moresby and Wyatt would be friends.

"And how was he, Miss Keane?"

"Interesting," she replied. "And very loyal to you."

Moresby crushed out the Havana, drained his glass of port, and drifted off to sleep in the armchair. He dreamed of ghosts and friends, of enemies and events. But always there was a cage in which he was locked, and Quittenden seemed to be all round the cage, laughing.

Chapter Nineteen

Sam woke me with coffee at just after eleven on Sunday morning. She was being the perfect P.A., looking after the guests and eventually remembering about me.

"Caswell called. Said thank you for the presents he found this morning. Between firearms charges and a wanted notice on Schmidt from Paris it should add up to ten years. He won't allow them to contact anyone for seventy-two hours."

I eased myself up and took the coffee cup. She sat on the edge of the bed and looked at me.

"Who's the lady?" she asked. "You've come back from London, obviously sleepless, and she calls you at odd hours."

"I thought we agreed. No ties, free agents and all that," I replied.

"Curious, that's all."

"Someone I met, a spook by profession. I'm still working out what her game is."

"Aha, seduced by a Mata Hari. Will they send the photographs under plain cover?"

I threw a pillow at her.

An hour later, I looked from the study window to see Siân Lewis leaning on the paddock railings, watching the horses, so I walked down and joined her. She turned her head, and I could see she'd been crying.

"Do you like horses?" I asked.

"Yes. You know where you are with them, not like people."

I could not fault the girl's logic. She was quiet for a moment, looking into the paddock.

"Daddy was going to buy me a horse, the day he was killed. I heard him and Mummy talking. Now he's gone. I'll never see him again."

I thought she was going to burst into tears. I was wrong. She had probably done all her crying—alone.

"I'm sorry for what I said to you—about my father. I didn't understand. I don't understand any of it."

"Don't be sorry." I smiled.

"That man last night frightened me. Thank God you came. You frightened me too. He won't come here, will he?"

"I doubt it. He's got more sense than that. Do you ride horses?"

"Yes." She smiled eagerly.

"What are you waiting for then? Let's go and find the man to find you a horse."

Graham Morgan was filling water buckets down at the stables. Sixteen, dark-haired, athletic, son of my farm's manager, he was too big to be a jockey. But the stables at Ty Newydd were his province. I'd bought them with the house; horses were a pleasant pastime for weekend visitors. Aberinvest had started sponsorship of sport, Fallon's idea. Graham was a good horseman and beginning to make a name for himself in equestrian circles.

I could see his eyes sparkle as I introduced Siân Lewis. She looked a lot older than fourteen.

"You look after her, young man. You know you've got to be very careful with my girlfriends."

He grinned. Siân Lewis smiled. Maybe I was making a friend.

I walked back toward the house.

The Khan brothers, Genghis and Kublai, were bounding across the lawns, playing with Ann Lewis' dog. I rounded a line of fir trees, and Ann Lewis cannoned straight into me. I caught her before she fell; she had shrieked surprise. I stood there for a second, holding her, and watching the dark pools of eyes. There was a quality about this woman that fascinated me. She made no attempt to move, and said nothing.

I heard a snarling noise behind me, then another to my left. The two enormous Dobermans were crouched, ready for action. I slowly let Ann Lewis go.

"Friend," I announced. "Remember me?"

The dogs stood, then wagged tails at me before bounding off to play again.

"I see you've met some of the defence force."

"Yes," she replied. "Frank Price introduced us this morning. Magnificent dogs."

"You won't have any trouble warding off strangers."

We walked through the grounds, through the north wood toward Home Farm, the Khan brothers and their playmate never far away.

"I left your daughter over at the stables. She's being looked after."

"She'll like that. We were going to see a horse for her the day David—" She broke off. "Sorry."

She controlled the grief. I admired this girl. Thinking back on it, Ty Newydd was perhaps not the easiest place for her to be.

"Siân told me."

"I don't know now, though. Have to see what Arthur Roberts says. He's putting David's affairs in order, as they say."

"You won't have any problems."

She stopped and stood in front of me. Maybe I'd said the wrong thing. Her eyes blazed for a second.

"We're not your problem, Mr. Wyatt. I appreciate what you've done but—"

"Women who argue annoy me," I interrupted her. "Now tell me about you while we walk back. I always take at least four sherries before Sunday lunch, large ones."

Maybe it was the way I said it. She burst out laughing. Then I laughed. I hadn't done much laughing of late, and I didn't suppose she had, either.

It turned out that Eustace Souter was reading the first lesson at evensong in a parish church outside Basingstoke. By all accounts a large, jovial, rubbery man of round-faced pleasantness, he exuded respectability, charity, and affluence. His house was a large, detached, architect-designed, local-stonework edifice that blended into the tranquillity of an acre of wooded ground outside the village of Basing, surrounded by thick hedges and reached by an unclassified lane. Information received advised me that the Souter family was holidaying in Ireland and that business complexities had prevented Père Souter from accompanying them. Nevertheless, he had attended church, placed his usual £10 note in the collection dish, and spoken outside with the vicar, chairwoman of the W.I., and Mrs. Knox-Allison, local fount of energy for all good causes.

I reflected that the £10 Souter had donated was earned in less than five minutes by one of his pushers in Piccadilly Circus, or in less than ten by one of his better quality call girls. I dislike hypocrites and despise religious hypocrites. Half the trouble in the world is caused by vicars in one shape or another. Eustace Souter had never been arrested, let alone prosecuted, for any criminal offence. Johnny's information reckoned him the foxiest and second nastiest villain in the country. More than one lady of the night had been scarred or

140

worse by his employees for cheating on her cash returns. Every day brought another hopeless and addicted loser on to his list of customers for narcotic drugs.

His family thought he ran a property business in the city. Friends and neighbours respected his generosity, sincerity, and hospitality. The metropolitan police suspected his involvement in nefarious activities. Numerous target operations had come to naught, for a variety of reasons, from information leaked to pressure brought.

Midnight on Sunday was a chilly time as we prepared to go in. The local police patrols had passed the Souter residence and were not due for another two hours at least. Johnny had one of his Hungarian chums driving the dark green transit van. He, Ko, and I were ready.

At 1:05 A.M. we moved. The Alsatian that guarded the rear door suffered a dart from Ko's blowpipe and fell into oblivion. Two hours later the dog would wake with a nasty taste in his mouth. That left the minder Souter had imported for the weekend, and the two girls who had arrived at the house at ten-fifteen in a Ferrari. They hadn't looked like the daily help.

The house was in darkness except for a bay-windowed room downstairs, which was heavily curtained and double-glazed. Johnny hit the telephone wires and burglar alarms while I let down the Ferrari's tyres and swiped the ignition keys someone had carelessly left in it. The only other vehicle around was Souter's XJS Jaguar parked in the garage, which was unlocked. I disconnected the distributor lead, pulled back the outer core of the cable, cut it, replaced the core, and connected up again.

Meanwhile Johnny had entered the house via the back door. I followed him to the kitchen, where cups were being rattled.

The minder was a big fellow, as big as Johnny, and he stood staring in disbelief at me for a split second. It's not every day a hooded man in combat gear with a .357 Magnum walks up and says good evening. Then Johnny took him out the way only Johnny can, with a sword-edged jab to the neck. The minder had managed one right-handed punch, but a hard-nosed villain is no match for a professional combat-trained killer. He collapsed, and Johnny cuffed him with the plastic cuffs, took his shoes, and dumped them in the kitchen waste bin.

I moved to cover the exit door, but I needn't have bothered. We could hear music coming from another room, the kind of music that you play when the girlfriend is coming round and the wife has gone to see her mother.

Eustace Souter had the money and bad taste of a provincial bookmaker. The hallway was hung with second-rate Art Nouveau, the carpet mock Persian, and it didn't match the wallpaper. A door across the hallway was open slightly, the lighting was low, and the music started upbeat.

I went through first. Always lead from the front. At least that way you never have to face the embarrassment of getting your arse shot off. There was no need to worry. Souter was otherwise engaged.

In front of a mock log fire, on two sheepskin rugs, was a tangle of writhing limbs which emitted gasping sounds. I couldn't make out who was doing what to whom or with what, but if I'd been in the hard-porn business I'd've had a field day. They were all as naked as the day they were born, and in Souter's case just as ugly. The women started screaming and disentangling themselves. Souter's language became very un-Christian.

"Shut up. Do as you're told, no one gets hurt. Eustace, stay where you are. Ladies—on the sofa."

The women stopped screaming. One was hardly more than fifteen, an innocent-looking kid with white skin and long blond hair. The other was older, short-cropped dark hair, all over suntan. She had hard eyes and a determined jaw line, and the complexion of a hooker. She recovered her composure and watched as Johnny cuffed Souter's pudgy hands behind his flabby frame.

142

"You fellows want some too?" She stood, hands on hips, pelvis gyrating slowly in what she imagined to be a provocative gesture.

"Put some clothes on." I indicated a pile of clothing on one of the armchairs. "Blondie, come here."

The kid was scared. She walked toward me uncertainly at first, then making up her mind, walked straight at me and didn't stop until her body touched mine.

"How old are you?"

"Young enough," she replied.

She already had the street-wise confidence of a survivor in a rough game, the business of life. I was holding the gun, but she was trading.

"You want to screw me?" she asked, voice pitched artificially low. "I'm a good girl. Do anything you want, anything."

She started moving her hands over me. I have seen a few bar girls in a lot of low places the world over, but this one was hardly more than a child. And the pupils of her green eyes were dilated. She was high as a kite on something. And it was not booze. I thought about childhood, about children, about games of hopscotch and hockey, about crushes on boyfriends and ice cream, and village fêtes and discos, about pet dogs and pop star posters. I looked at the girl and could see none of those—only numbed senses, no feeling—the worst kind of exploitation.

I took her hand, pushed her over to the sofa.

"Clothes, now."

Meanwhile Souter had been babbling, called for his minder, blustered, threatened. I had seen the girl. Now I wanted to do a clog dance on his head. I walked toward him, dragged him into a chair, and hated that flabby man of round-faced righteousness. He was blustering now.

"I'll have you done for this, you bastards."

I cocked the Magnum and let the muzzle of the silencer rest on his top lip, pointing up his nose. I tried very hard to remember there was only an ounce of trigger pull on its single action. What I had seen, what he'd tried to do to Ann and Siân Lewis, made it very easy for me to forget.

"Your minder is out. The grounds are covered, communications cut," I said coldly. "Who paid you to send Schmidt and Klausen after two women called Lewis?"

"I—"

The muzzle pressed hard against his nose. The bluster was gone, the eyes popping in horror.

"I don't know the principal. I was the agent. Instructions arrived by phone, photographs and drawings by letter. I don't know . . ."

He began blubbering.

"What else? Done any work for this man before?"

"Y-Yes. A man called Osborne, a journalist."

"When?"

"December last year. Osborne was killed."

"How did this man find you?"

"Said he was recommended, by Samuelson."

"Who's Samuelson?"

"New Yorker. But Samuelson didn't know him. Then he said he'd heard about one of my operations. If I didn't do the contract he'd blow me. I said no, and the next day the police raided my warehouse. I was lucky to stay out of it. Then he called again, said kill Osborne. So I did. He paid up, over the odds."

"What does Samuelson do in New York?"

"Cosa Nostra—New York godfather."

I could see his brain registering I was no villain or I'd know my way around.

"When did these instructions to kill the Lewises arrive?"

"Thursday night, by phone, then Friday morning, special messenger, with the photos and money."

"Which service?"

"Don't know." He shook his head.

"That's all I need from you."

I stood back, ten feet, levelled the gun at him. He was blub-

144

bering again for mercy, anything I wanted, there was money in the desk in the next room. I nodded to Johnny, who came back with a fistful of ten-pound notes. He gagged Souter and the black-haired harridan and tied them back to back on the floor. I beckoned to the girl, who by now had put on a white T-shirt, jeans, and sandals.

"You come with us."

I let Johnny lead her out. Then I turned as I left the room.

"Eustace. Make one move against the Lewises, or try to trace me, and I'll be back, when you least expect me, wherever you are—and I'll kill you."

We were clear of the area within fifteen minutes. No screaming of tyres or racing away or any other kind of histrionics, just a quiet leisurely drive within speed limits to London. I stopped off half an hour after we left Souter and called the police, and told them where they could find certain noxious substances as defined by the Dangerous Drugs Act. I knew because I had put them there. Whatever else the cops found was their problem.

The blond girl was a different story. I didn't want her wandering around London in her condition, so I called an acquaintance who runs a clinic in Paris and got her booked in for the cure. We had lifted five and a half grand from Souter—careless of him to leave money lying around. I contacted Gareth Dane, London's most reliable security agency boss, and had him accompany the girl to Paris, with the money and instructions to a friend of mine in the French government service. Little technicalities like immigration and identity can be disposed of when you know the right people.

I was in the Park Lane flat by 3 A.M. I owned the property under an alias. Fallon used it from time to time for short-stay foreign business contacts he wanted to keep away from the press. I also suspected him for using it on occasion to meet other people's wives. I had suspected that the security services might be tapping the phones at the Aberinvest flat. They could have done the same at Ty Newydd, so conversations were guarded. But the Park Lane address was untraceable to me, and we had not been followed.

Johnny poured two large malts. I sat in the darkened lounge watching the lights and traffic, smoked a thin Havana and tried to put it all together. I had the hypothesis that Moresby was framed. And I had hired killers running around the place, with no one knowing who had sent them. This business was going to get dirtier, very soon. If that was possible. I wished the Mossad would find Said. Maybe his employer had already found him, which would be the end of the only trail I had. Maybe that would satisfy Said's employer. Maybe he would leave the Lewises alone, and let me go back fishing. I tried telling myself that because I wanted to hear it.

There was a risk factor. Said's employer was powerful. He knew the moves. Maybe he would kill Ann Lewis and me just to be doubly safe. There's an old Arab custom that says if you save a person's life, you're responsible for it. And I felt responsible for the Lewises. There is another old saying: Do unto others before they do it unto you.

It was waiting time now. And who-to-trust time. The Mossad had to come up with Nury al Said within twenty-four hours, or Moresby could be in more trouble, legal trouble, like being charged under the Official Secrets Act.

Unless certain powers thought he ought to have an accident.

I went to bed, tired but unable to sleep. So I watched the traffic, and the lights, and tried not to worry too much about what the day would bring. What bothered me most was the message from Isser Bar Lev's computer. The Mossad's best bet on Moresby's antagonist was the K.G.B.

I've mixed with the best of them in my time, but I've never fought a state within a state that controls the state. It looked like we were outnumbered, about ten thousand to one. But the Spartans, all three hundred of them, held off those kind of odds at Thermopylae. Until someone showed the Persians the back way round the mountains.

146

Chapter Twenty————————————

I did not get to sleep. There was an insistent ringing at the doorbell. At 5:10 A.M. it was too early for the milkman.

Johnny was there, ready, .45 in hand.

"Bird, long dark hair, early twenties, jeans, and jacket. Looks your type," he called.

I looked at the monitor screen.

"Mossad," I replied. "Let her in."

Johnny was wary. He closed the door behind her and started to frisk her.

"Tell this ape to get his hands off me," she demanded.

"He has the best of intentions," I apologized. "Coffee or a drink?"

"No time for that." She was a very businesslike lady. "Now, I am Ruth, this thing here is called Johnny, and you are Wyatt. The man has your merchandise. I want your word you won't kill him, or try to remove him."

"I won't kill him. But a policeman I know wants to present him with a set of handcuffs."

She looked indecisive for a second.

"The man will decide. You want to see him?"

I nodded.

"Wyatt comes alone," she told Johnny.

"Don't like it," he replied. "You've got Wyatt. Say the man has done a deal with someone."

The girl's eyes flashed anger. She tossed the mane of dark flowing hair and responded, voice low and furious.

"Our people know what it is for their lives to be bartered. The man would not do such a thing."

"You're beautiful when you're cross." Johnny smiled. "How about dinner sometime, I—"

She looked at him disdainfully.

"I don't date old men. Wyatt, we waste time. Give grandfather your gun."

"I'm not carrying."

"But he'd like you to search him," Johnny quipped.

"You two should be in a theatre," she replied. "An operating theatre."

Outside, I was put in the back of a transit with darkened windows. For twenty minutes the van bumped around. The back suspension needed attention. So did the interior. Its last cargo had been chickens. The smell was vile. I lit a Havana to mollify the insult to my nasal senses. Then the van came to a halt and I heard doors being pulled shut.

They were taking no chances. I was let out in a garage and led through a doorway down cold-sounding steps into a basement that was dark round the edges and dimly lit in the middle by a forty-watt bulb hanging from a single flex. The room smelt damp and mouldy and as the door closed behind me, the stench of stale urine and sick hit me like a gust of cold wind.

A short, bearded man in shirt-sleeves and sports trousers leaned back against one wall on a rickety chair. Slung around his neck was an Uzi submachine gun pointed toward an old bedstead in one corner of the room. The clicking sound as he played with the safety catch made me uncomfortable. If Isser Bar Lev had trapped me, I had no chance.

Strapped firmly to the bed was a gaunt, dishevelled man, lying on a filthy mattress. The brown eyes just gazed at me with no perception. Nury al Said was in conditions you wouldn't keep an animal. They'd obviously been talking to him. He had the pallor of wasting death. It was a fair bet he was full of scopolamine or sodium pentothal or whatever the fashionable truth serum was these days.

148

I could have felt sorry for him, lying there like human waste, a sacrificial offering to the depths of a man's cruelty. Then I thought about Ann Lewis, the horror she had lived through, and I did not feel quite so sorry for the bastard anymore. So I chain-lit another Havana and concentrated my mental faculties on the task at hand.

"Remember me?" I asked.

After about thirty seconds, recognition registered in the eyes.

"What are you going to do?" The voice was a hoarse, throaty vibration. He looked at the girl, then at me.

"Who sent you?" I demanded.

He shook his head slowly. Maybe he was coming out from the effects of the drug. Ruth produced a syringe from nowhere and seized his arm. I held her back, shook my head. She was angry.

"You want to know," she argued. "This is the only way."

"He's half-dead already."

"He tried to kill you."

There was no answer to that. She didn't wait for one, but shot Said full of dope again.

"I'll leave you with them," I announced.

"They will kill me." His voice surged in protest, but the sounds were no louder.

"Slowly," Ruth replied. "As your friends have killed us."

I waited for the reply.

"My instructions came as usual."

"Go on," Ruth ordered.

And he did. At great length. Nury al Said spilled out of a scrambled brain every detail he could remember. His instructor was unknown, but the times they were given and the exact method of payment for the contract on David Lewis were clear. The same method had been employed in two previous killings Nury had undertaken. He elaborated, dates, times, and names. One was an M.I.5 operative in West Berlin on January 28. The other was an American journalist who had died in a car accident outside Lyons on March 21. The car had been tampered with by an expert. The police had no suspicions. All the time he talked, a tape recorder ran. Two hours after I had first entered the basement, Moresby's treachery had infinite possibilities, and repercussions.

I bade Nury al Said good day.

"Don't leave me," he whispered. "Don't."

I walked on; Ruth followed me.

"Ruth, keep him alive and off the dope."

"We no longer require him," she replied. "He has told us all he can. The man will speak with you."

She was a hard lady, beautiful but vicious. Something had made her that way.

"Where are you from?" I asked.

"Kibbutz Nahalia . . . you remember? You were there. You saw the bodies of my family. You saw three children who had buried themselves in the sand to escape the Fedayeen."

I did not need reminding. Those border-hopping cutthroats made Eichmann and Mengele look like saints.

"I was one of those children, Wyatt. I have learned to fight for myself now."

She spoke the words slowly, deliberately.

I then understood why. And why the killing never stops.

I did not feel much like breakfast. But I had information and needed more information. At 8:21 A.M. I called Vicky Keane, and became slightly excited at the sound of that Roedean voice. It was who-do-we-trust time. I knew a good place for a late breakfast and met her there at nine-o-three.

She had too much class to work for whoever it was she worked for in that murky, dirty, double-dealing world that I had left barely two hours before in a filthy basement somewhere in this city. I watched her walk in, with style, the red hair cascading over a thin white summer dress with a neckline just low enough to be interesting. Her eyes laughed, the lustrous lips smiled, and I wondered where she was hiding the .25.

150

She ate a grapefruit, three thin slices of ham, and drank black coffee. I walloped two gammon steaks, mushrooms, eggs, and toast.

"Thanks for Sunday," she announced. "I've been trying to contact you since last night."

"What happened?"

"Sunday was on-the-carpet day. I'm on assignment to Q, who seems to have the business of evaluating Moresby well in hand. He was jagged angry about our not bringing the Lewises in. Anyway, I was sent to talk to Moresby, to chat generally and to throw in odd names, like yours, ask odd questions from Q's brief. Moresby kept looking at me. I'm sure his mind was somewhere else. In fact I had the feeling he thought he was talking to a ghost, as if I was not really who I seemed. Probably sounds silly to you."

"No. You remind him of Elise." Moresby had told me once, in a moment of careless reminiscence over sherry at Ty Newydd one Christmas. We had both been discussing the fact that everyone had gone home—it was late Christmas Eve. Only Frank was on duty in the security room. The log fire was blazing. A Christmas tree stood in the corner of a room that was empty except for the two of us. There was no laughter, no sound of children, no hushed excitement at presents being wrapped. Then he told me the story of Elise.

I recounted a brief version to Vicky Keane, who listened quietly. When I had finished she lit a cigarette.

"That Q must be a cruel, unfeeling bastard," she announced.

"Doing his job," I replied. "But Moresby will never forgive him for it."

I changed the subject to ask for information about the killings Said had confessed to. She noted times and dates.

"Where did you get this?" she asked.

"From a man."

"Why don't you trust me?" she asked. "I want the truth, too."

"I don't tell anyone what you've told me," I replied.

"I'm putting my job on the line. Doesn't that deserve consideration? In fact, I am guilty of conspiracy under the Act."

"Everyone in this game is guilty of conspiracy. If I tell you, you have to pass the information to Q. Just for a change I'd like to be one step ahead in this mess. I promise you'll be the first to know."

"This is very heavy stuff, Wyatt. We spooks don't kill each other frequently—that is a popular misconception. Carl Morgan of Five was hit as a last resort, in a hotel room in Berlin. Rumour was, he had turned a very senior Czech Intelligence officer and was getting him out. The home run was planned for the night Morgan was hit. The Czech never showed. I was backup for resources from the London end. Calladyne and two others assisted, but weren't in on the why."

"Who got him?"

"We never found out for certain. I thought it was K.G.B. But S.I.S. put in a report that Czech Intelligence had covered their man and hit Morgan as a warning. It was not playing the game, but they have not done it since. Top-level warnings were issued. We don't kill each other."

"Who knew Morgan had turned his man?"

"Only senior level. S.I.S. from D.Ops upward—that's four men. And Moresby. We weren't told who was coming out."

"Would they have known?"

"S.I.S. would."

"Would the K.G.B. or Czech Intelligence use contract killers?"

"You do know something," she mused.

I waited for her answer.

"No. For that kind of operation they'd use their own best men. And Centre hoods are very, very good."

"Would your senior people have known this Czech's identity?"

"Almost certainly."

"Why use M.I.5?"

"Morgan was the contact. His mother was Czech. That's the story I heard, anyway."

"You're a communicative lot, between each other. Now on March twenty-first an American journalist called Travanti died in a car accident outside Lyons. Can you find out who he really was, who he worked for, and on what?"

"Tall order. How long have I got?"

"Yesterday. But be careful not to make too much noise about it. Need to know, or whatever. Make sure you're not tailed."

"I'll play it very close," she promised.

"And I'll come and collect you at eight for dinner."

"I'd like that."

I kissed her au revoir.

The threads were beginning to come together. Something appallingly simple but devastating was going on. Something rotten in the state of security had occurred. Moresby's arrest and the ensuing chaos was nothing compared to what could happen. I hoped my fertile imagination was running wild. Had I told anyone responsible they would have committed me to an asylum. Or probably had me killed on the spot.

I saw Johnny back at the flat. Vicky Keane had memorized my new phone number so that was out for operational calls. My Hungarian chum did not look happy. I did not wait for him to tell me what he had been up to. When I'd finished my speculation he looked worried.

"I don't go with your ideas. They're possible, but—on the other hand, we've got trouble."

"What?"

He lit a Gauloise and put a black coffee in front of me.

"Alexei Svetkin is in London."

The name meant nothing to me.

"He's the number-two man, or so rumour has it, in Moscow Centre. Last time he left Moscow, somebody hit Reagan.

Time before that it was the Saudi oil minister. This guy is not just dangerous. He's lethal. They call him the surgeon. I told you there were two identified K.G.B. goons in London already; well, they've dropped out of sight. Who knows who else is around."

"You are worried."

I watched his open-cast features. They betrayed no emotion. He lit another Gauloise and walked to the window.

"Wyatt, I'm more than worried. I'm scared stiff. Everyone I spoke to this morning said Svetkin is here and then ran like hell."

"Could they be after émigrés? Anyone causing a nuisance?"

"The surgeon only goes for the big one that people speculate about years after, write books about, make films about."

"Leaves me out." I smiled. "I'm not famous or a president, or—"

"It's you or Moresby. Has to be."

"He could be after anyone," I insisted. "Perhaps he's come to pay homage at Highgate or stand for leadership of the Labour party."

"Gut feeling says we're part of it."

"Recommendations?" I demanded.

"Six months' vacation. Acapulco."

Johnny was serious. Suddenly my jokes were not amusing. When a man like Johnny starts worrying about his safety it's time to take out more life insurance and seek healthier climes. I left the coffee and poured myself a stiff malt. Booze is no solution to a problem, but it gives your nervous hands something to do. You momentarily feel warm and comfortable inside.

I had always been the planner, the strategist, the tactician. My job was now to plan us out of the mess. Johnny had the perfect solution, a very tempting solution.

"You take the plane," I said, finally.

He was silent for a moment, then asked, "And you?"

"If you are correct in your assumption, I think I'll stick

around for a while, see if this surgeon fellow is as good as he's made out to be."

The granite face grinned, then he burst out laughing.

"Suppose we can always go to Acapulco next year, Wyatt."

If there was a next year.

Chapter Twenty-one————————

The meeting had been set for 9 A.M. on Monday, August 30. The fine weather had broken earlier into cloud and showers of light rain. The three men, Quittenden, Lansbury, and Llewellyn Jones, had gathered in Quittenden's offices at Lancaster Gate. Llewellyn Jones and Quittenden had already been together for more than an hour, listening to tapes of Sir Philip Moresby's conversations.

Lansbury felt uncomfortable, as the last man into a meeting always does. Had they been talking about him? What was the real purpose of the meeting? He had spent several days wondering about his position. What action was Quittenden going to recommend about his non-communication of Moresby's admission that he had been seeing the Libyan, Colonel Abdul Fahd?

They had taken coffee, but Quittenden ordered more for Lansbury, who sat uncomfortably on the steel-framed chair. The computer screens seemed to Lansbury to watch his every move, as if they were an extension of their controller's personality. Quittenden and Llewellyn Jones went on reading typescripts and casting each other occasional glances, like two magistrates who had already decided the punishment of the accused, but had to keep up the appearance of weighing the evidence. Lansbury had seen it as a policeman.

155

The secretary brought the coffee. Lansbury smiled his thanks and she smiled back. He watched the swinging hips and long, leather boots and wondered if Quittenden was giving her anything. Somehow he could not imagine Quittenden with a woman.

"Richard," Quittenden finally addressed him. "Why do you think Alexei Svetkin is in London?"

"Up to no good." Lansbury puffed on his pipe. "He has not moved from the Embassy since he arrived. Cheltenham reports increased radio traffic to Centre. Could be he's in charge of Moresby's recovery. I can't see what else is going on. Nothing on the books to justify his intervention."

Llewellyn Jones nodded agreement.

"I think they are going to cheat on the deal," Quittenden observed. "L.J.'s people at the F.C.O. have been making agreeable noises about exchanging Moresby. Centre is beginning to press for a date. We'll run it another week or two before committing ourselves to a definite date, and acceptance or refusal. But I think they might try to grab him for free."

Lansbury shook his head.

"Can't see it. Can I ask why?"

"Saves them handing our agent back. Gives them tremendous propaganda value. Also saves any network Moresby's been using."

Lansbury had to agree they were three good reasons.

"I'll double the watch on him, if that's the case."

"Where is he?" asked Llewellyn Jones noncommittally.

"Esher," Lansbury replied. "My lads have him under wraps and a four-man guard."

Llewellyn Jones looked at Quittenden.

"I think a move, Q."

Quittenden nodded.

"We'll use a safe house I have. On the Gower, in West Wales. It's set back a bit, in its own grounds. I'll arrange for S.A.S. cover. You'll be contacted about transportation details later, Richard. Cover it personally, will you?"

Lansbury nodded. Quittenden and Llewellyn Jones went back

to their transcripts, and Lansbury decided he was no longer required.

His Rover car waited outside. On the drive back to his office he could not work out the ideas those two men had. Sometimes they involved him to the hilt; at others, left him in the dark. But he had enough to worry about.

At the same time, in a room deep in the basement of what appeared to be an ordinary house, a shirt-sleeved man called Alpha looked at a computer screen and smiled to himself. He entered a note in a small black book and went back to reading a very thin document.

Alexei Svetkin took a leisurely breakfast at 8:03 A.M. on Monday, August 29, and listened to Second Assistant Secretary Vladimir Baikal's excuses. Svetkin lit his first cigarette of the day and his eyes rested on the unfortunate Baikal.

"Keep trying, Comrade," he added neutrally, neither malice nor warmth in his voice. "Although now someone else has him we can restructure our plans."

Baikal felt Svetkin could be annoyed about that.

"I may go out later. I do not want an escort."

This time the voice was cold.

Baikal was about to protest. Station procedure demanded that his superior be covered at all times. But Baikal was not about to compound his errors by arguing the point. So he left the room and instructed two cultural attachés to watch over Comrade Svetkin from a discreet distance. . . .

It was not until 11 A.M. that Svetkin left the Embassy. He was followed, but fifteen minutes later disappeared from his watchdogs in Kensington Gore. There had also been other watchers. British security, Svetkin had surmised. A supreme master of streetcraft, he walked along the Kensington Road and slipped unobserved into a phone box. He dialled a number, let it ring three times, and replaced the receiver. Twice he repeated the operation. Within a minute of his replacing the receiver a third time, the instrument rang.

"We must meet. One hour," he announced and replaced the receiver.

He walked on, into Piccadilly. Then he constantly changed direction, stopped in a public house for a malt whisky and watched the early lunchtime drinkers. He continued his progress toward Victoria Station, stopping, changing direction, entering and leaving shops by different entrances and directions. He played the game as only he knew how. He was about to bring off the biggest coup of his career. Operation Nimrod was his brainchild.

At Victoria Station he met his contact of long acquaintance. A man had no friends in this business. Although they had met on only two previous occasions, each was vital to the other's interest. But they had no personal feelings for each other.

"You have not found Said," Svetkin stated.

"So who has him?" the contact asked.

"Not important now. I have decided to finish the interference."

"I also have a problem. There is a leak."

"Close it. No more freelance or criminals," Svetkin warned.

"I need your best men, now."

"Call this number. Code Nimrod. I have two there waiting."

"And the interference can be closed at the same time."

"We need to be sure. I will want to see. We will both have to see." Svetkin did not smile, but walked on.

Richard Lansbury telephoned Quittenden at 2:35 P.M. Svetkin had returned to the Embassy at 2:07 P.M. Quittenden was not angry. He was apoplectic. Lansbury had never heard the man in such a mood. He did not believe the cool Quittenden could ever be capable of such emotion.

"Lansbury, take the bloody Brigade of Guards if you have to. I want Moresby safely in that location and secure from anything up to and including a nuclear attack. Do you understand?"

"Yes," Lansbury replied, and sent for the two watchers who had lost Svetkin. They stood before him, suitably abashed.

158

"Let's see if we can keep our eyes open this time, shall we?" Lansbury invited angrily. "I want three cars and the van. Everyone tooled up, out front in five minutes. Move it."

Thirty minutes later, Richard Lansbury walked into Sir Philip Moresby's room. Moresby was sitting in the armchair. He rose and offered Lansbury a sherry. Lansbury accepted and sat down.

"We're moving you, Philip."

"I had gathered by all the activity," Moresby replied.

Lansbury thought Moresby seemed concerned. The dry sense of humour was still there, but the confidence seemed to be shaken slightly.

"To somewhere safer, I presume. Q's orders?"

Lansbury nodded.

"Don't suppose you'd do me a favour, would you Dick? For old times' sake."

"What's that Philip?" Lansbury asked casually.

"Tell Wyatt where you've taken me. And make sure we're not ambushed on the way."

Lansbury puzzled over the request for a moment.

"No to the first, yes to the second."

"Some comfort in that, I suppose." Moresby drained his glass, stood up with the brave resignation of a man about to meet a firing squad, and walked out through the door.

Lansbury knew that he could lose his job by complying with the first request. To comply with the second was to do his job. Sir Philip Moresby had given some strange orders in his time, but none stranger than the last words he had uttered to Lansbury. So he joined Sir Philip in the rear of an armoured secruity van, and spoke a string of orders into his handset.

The four-vehicle convoy moved off. It was 4:05 P.M.

Alexei Svetkin took no lunch. He returned to the Yellow Room at 2:15 P.M. and took with him a box of Havana cigars.

The two men he had detailed to report to his contact called in; Svetkin thought, quickly. He ordered them to carry out the instructions his contact had given them. Reports of M.I.5 activity were coming in to him. He sat back, lit a cigar, and swung himself around in the swivel chair.

All he had to do now was wait. The computer chess game he programmed would occupy his time until the word came in: Interference on Operation Nimrod terminated.

Chapter Twenty-two———————

Vicky Keane called me at 2:45 P.M.

"Can we meet immediately?" she asked.

"Sure."

"Bayswater Road end of the Serpentine in half an hour."

"See you."

The receiver clicked down. She had sounded pleased. Maybe the lady spook had something for me. I told Johnny.

"Not happy. Could be a setup."

"So I'll take a gun."

I clipped the .357 Magnum to my waist, butt forward, left-hand side. I put on the blazer and adjusted my tie.

"I'll walk. If you think we're in trouble, follow me, on foot. Have the Rolls stand by at the Bayswater Road end and chance the parking tickets."

"Watch out," Johnny warned.

I crossed Park Lane and the East Carriage Road. The weather had cleared and the sun shone bright and warm. Everyone else was walking in shirt-sleeves or lolling on the grass or sunbathing. I kept my eyes open, changed direction a couple of times, and was at my destination in twenty-five minutes.

When you're suspicious of being hunted, you get a funny feeling. Every movement made by every passerby seems sinister. You read motives into the most innocent actions—a man looking in his pocket for cigarettes—a middle-aged lady delving into her shopping bag—a young mother tucking clothes around a baby in a pram. You watch the eyes that might be watching you, the glances that are not for you, and the blank stares you get in return because they are watching you watching them and wondering why. If you're not careful you can get arrested.

Vicky Keane was late at 3:30 P.M.; by 4:00 P.M. she was overdue. I was edgy. I'd been propositioned twice—once by a frizzy-haired female with nipples showing under a thin T-shirt that proclaimed Women's Lib—"Make him sleep in the wet patches." I guessed she was trying out her femininity and declined the offer, and that was before I'd read the slogan. The second was by a middle-aged, grey-tinted queer wearing a white felt hat and tight jeans. I flipped open my wallet, showed him my old security pass and told him to move before I arrested him. He had not looked too closely at the pass because he was ten yards away by the time the wallet had flipped open. One of nature's survivors. Four black kids who had been watching me saw the proceedings and shuffled off. I just hoped there were no real cops lurking in the vicinity.

Johnny wandered across at 4:10 P.M. and smiled.

"We've been stood up."

"Or she's in trouble," I replied.

"How did she sound on the phone?"

"Okay."

"Where did she call from?"

"Didn't say. Look, find Carson, grab the Rolls. Leave him here. He knows what she looks like. You can drive."

It took another ten minutes before we were on our way. Johnny broke every speed limit in the book getting to Vicky Keane's basement flat on the Cromwell Road. I was first down the steps, almost falling over a fleetfooted tabby cat. I dodged the empty milk bottles and pressed the doorbell next to the speaker.

I got no verbal reply, but the door opened automatically. I have an unpleasant tickling sensation that affects the nape of my neck when there is trouble likely to involve me. No one believes me, but it's true. I had it as the door opened. The downstairs curtains were closed, but they had been when I took her back to the flat. I wished I had taken her inside then, so at least I would know the layout on the other side of the door. That door had not opened very far, and what I could see of the room was in darkness.

I signalled to Johnny. He jumped across to the other side of the doorway.

"Hello," I called.

There was no reply. The door stayed motionlessly ajar. I leaned over, grabbed the dustbin lid, and half a dozen wasps greeted me. Johnny nodded.

There is never an easy way to do it. Fast is the best way. And fast it was. I chucked the dustbin lid through the door.

An ear-shattering blast replied. Someone had fired two shotgun barrels simultaneously. Lead and chipped stonework ricocheted around the place as Johnny dived through the doorway to the right, rapid-firing the big .45. I went left and a gun flash spurted from the darkness, thirty feet away. I fired twice, the Magnum jerking upward, and I rolled left-ward again, crashing against a table. The noise echoed that of a body being smashed against furniture.

Further inside came the noise of two shots, one a light gun like a .25, the other bigger. Footsteps sounded. A door slammed. I did a stupid thing and rushed across the room toward another door. I was aware of another gun flash and the sucking sound of air being disturbed close to my head. Two more shots sounded as Johnny replied to the shot that had missed me by less than an inch. I had known it was a silly move, but I had to make it. The .25 shot had to be Vicky Keane. But I'd heard another shot, after hers.

Johnny had also moved fast. By the time I dived through the second door into a hallway, he was covering me. I pointed to an open back door, and dived through another open doorway on the other side of the hall. Johnny was on his way out as we heard a car engine being revved at high speed.

Someone had wrecked the room I was in. Books were scattered over the floor, curtains torn. Then I heard this low moaning noise, and saw Vicky Keane.

They had made a mess of her. The beautiful freckled face was battered and streaked with blood. The naked golden tanned body was crisscrossed with bloody scars. Her sparkling eyes were closing with massive bruises. In a broken right hand she held the .25. But there was a hole in her stomach from a bullet, oozing blood. It didn't look good. I caught her as she fell down again.

"Easy, baby, easy," I whispered. The eyes ran tears of fear.

"Johnny, ambulance fast," I called.

He looked around the doorway, saw me laying her on the unmade bed. She gripped my hands.

"Wyatt—" She struggled to speak. Every breath she uttered must have brought new torture to a pain-racked body.

"I saw Q," she moaned. "I saw Q—Morgan. Then this."

"Easy now. Don't talk."

I could not think clearly. All I could see was a broken mass of flesh and bone where a beautiful girl used to be. She raised herself in my arms.

"I love—you—Wyatt. Go get—"

She was dead. She was bloody dead, smashed to pieces. I held her, cradled her, tried to bring her back. But she had gone, tortured into oblivion. I was angry, lightheaded, sick, and full of hate—cold, silent hate. I don't know how long I was there. I rested her head on the pillow, arranged the deep red hair around her shoulders. I stood back silently. Behind me I heard footsteps. A voice said "Jesus Christ." Sounds of a man retching. Johnny's order: "Get him out of here."

All I could see was Vicky Keane, dead. I felt cold, abysmally empty as though I were falling for eternity through an endless space. God knows how long I stood there. The picture of horror encircled me, pressed on my brain.

I took my jacket off and covered Vicky's face. I draped a dressing gown over the body and turned. Johnny was there, silent.

I walked through the devastated flat, pushing silently past policemen. The air in the lounge was acrid with cordite. No one stood in my way. I got outside. The street was crowded with people, flashing blue lights, and sirens. Two ambulance men stood, grey-faced, a stretcher propped by the door. More cars arrived. Men came running. I leaned against the Rolls. The scene was unreal. I did not take half of it in. Then Johnny was beside me, with another man I didn't know.

"They've contacted Lansbury. He's out of town. Says to get you out. He'll square it with the boys in blue."

I climbed into the Rolls. Johnny drove. He handed me a lighted Gauloise. I don't smoke cigarettes. I don't remember the drive back to Park Lane. All I could see was the room, and the girl, broken like a doll. And I remembered the words, words I will always have to live with.

I drank the first scotch automatically. My clothes were covered in blood, but I did not much care. I unholstered the Magnum, ejected the two empty shells, and held it in my hand.

I was going to kill the third man in that flat, and whoever had sent him.

Johnny just stood silently, watching me.

"I'm sorry, Wyatt."

"You're sorry," I snapped. "I sent her into that. She was helping me and they got to her. They used her to set us up and butchered her. Christ, Johnny, she was only a kid. What chance did she have? Tell me. Now get me a location on that Svetkin fellow. I'm going after him."

"No, sir," he replied. Johnny had not called me "sir" since the Six Day War.

"That's an order," I snapped.

"No, sir," his voice low, even threatening.

I turned to face him. He stood in his shirt-sleeves, white expanse crossed with straps from the leather shoulder holster, and the Colt resting against his left side. His eyes met mine. His granite face was impassive. I knew there would be more words.

"I know how you feel, Wyatt. Christ I know. For two pins I'd go down to Kensington Palace Gardens and brain the first Red asshole I could grab. They're expecting that. If you go off at half cock, they'll bury us. And I'd hate that little redhead to have died for nothing. She kept us alive by holding out there. She got a shot off when they'd killed her. She died to keep us in this game. Now let's stay in it. I never saw you tackle an operation unprepared and God we're going to need that planning. Lansbury is on his way up and he'll do some talking. Get that scotch down you, get washed up, and we'll get sorted. Then we'll plan it and show Comrade Svetkin how we kick K.G.B. ass."

We looked at each other. I could not fault his logic. It was what I should have thought. And Vicky Keane had spoken those words. In the next two hours I thought about those words.

Lansbury came at just after 7:30 P.M. We'd blown our cover on the flat but it did not matter now. They were running around town shooting people. We were about to move fast and give the bastards a running fight.

Richard Lansbury took a stiff slug of scotch. He wanted to know what had happened, so Johnny told him. I was making calls from the bedroom phone, and when I came in the room he just looked.

"Sorry, Wyatt." The mournful face was grey. "I just came from the mortuary."

"What are you doing about it?" I demanded.

"She was my agent, on secondment to another section. Officially it's their affair. Unofficially, I've got everyone out on the streets hassling every known source of information. What puzzles me is how you knew her."

"She wanted some photographs I'd taken of a couple of

plumbers. It developed from there, excuse the pun. She called me with something I wanted to know. I never got it."

He was thoughtful for a moment.

"She worked on this Moresby affair, I know." He spoke slowly, mostly to himself.

"You boys got it wrong. Moresby's not bent. Someone wants you to think he is. I don't trust any of you. For all I know your next call is to the K.G.B."

He stood up, angrily shouting.

"That's enough. You don't call me a traitor. It's not my operation."

"Dick, I want to know what goes on."

He almost threw his hands in the air.

"I don't bloody well know. Give me some time. I'll get back to you."

"No time left."

"Wyatt, stay out."

I shook my head. Lansbury stood up and walked to the door. Johnny had been quiet throughout the conversation, but as Lansbury passed him, Johnny said:

"Lansbury, listen a minute. I'm like you. I'm the hired help. I know what the problems are. But tell your chief this. You ain't dealing with young girls and expendable civilians now. Like you saw, me and Wyatt shoot back."

Chapter Twenty-three————————

By 11:00 P.M. on Monday, August 30, Alexei Svetkin was aware that Operation Nimrod had received a setback. Baikal's safe line had received a message to say that the interference had not been neutralized, and that two out of three operatives had. The third was in need of hospitalization for a .25-calibre bullet wound in the shoulder.

Svetkin had dined well on Beluga, filet de boeuf mignon, lemon surprise, and his favorite Camembert. He had spent an hour drinking Napoleon with the Ambassador and discussing the few current successes in Afghanistan. He did not need bad news to upset his digestion.

He could not risk communication with his contact. British security had acted swiftly in the wake of Vicky Keane's murder. M.I.5 and Special Branch were turning over every suspect address and had accidentally stumbled on a minor agent whose loss would prove irritating. Svetkin had guessed that the operation would provoke a certain reaction and was prepared to take the risk if success of Nimrod had been guaranteed. But the operation had been a failure. And he had lost two good men.

Just after midnight, the contact called into Baikal's safe line. Svetkin took control.

"You know the penalty of failure," he spoke softly.

"Said's alive and threatening to go to the police." The voice on the other end of the line was calm." Unless we take two hundred thousand pounds to him."

Svetkin thought rapidly.

"Location?"

"To follow in an hour."

"Can you trace the call?"

"No."

"It sounds wrong."

"I know it's wrong," the contact confirmed. "Said's not that stupid, or is he? I'll call in the location."

Svetkin turned to Baikal.

"I want every available man alerted. Get Yevshenko and Richman, and that German madman. He has a unit in London."

"I understood that was to be used for Black June," Baikal protested.

"Get it."

Svetkin turned to his computer console. These machines could do almost anything. But they could not tell you what a man was thinking. All about him, yes; but never what his thoughts were.

Svetkin put himself in his opposite's position. Tactical withdrawal, then attack from a defensive position, a running defence. Yes, he thought. I can see your game. It will be on open ground. Very well, we shall fight on open ground.

At 12:15 A.M. the call came from the contact.

"Wales," the contact confirmed. "Six A.M. in Wales, a dam, a place called Llyne Brianne, in the hills, near Llandovery—nearest town."

"Maps," Svetkin called out. His computer operator pressed buttons. Within seconds an ordnance survey appeared on two screens.

"I have it. Mountain country. Not a building for miles."

"There's a small hut by the lakeside." The contact continued with a map reference and some bad Welsh pronunciation.

"He's left time tight," the contact observed.

"So we get there first. Use a helicopter. Meet me at two A.M. Dawn is at five A.M. We will be in position before the time."

Svetkin gave the location and ordered Baikal to ready the men.

Baikal returned as Svetkin put on an overcoat and loaded a Makarov automatic.

"Comrade. You cannot be serious."

"Of course I am serious. I command this operation. I can suffer no further setbacks to Nimrod. You will remain here."

Simon Quittenden was dining at his flat with a Guyanese lady when Lansbury arrived at 8:31 P.M uninvited. Quittenden did not take kindly to the disturbance. Lansbury was in no mood to be bullied, even if it did cost him his job. Quittenden took him into a study and turned on him.

"I hope this is vital," he warned.

"I lost an agent. Keane. They did a real job on her."

Quittenden stood, wine glass in hand and said nothing. He just stared at Lansbury. Then:

"Keane was on secondment to an S.I.S. unit, my agent, not yours," he emphasized "Furthermore, Richard, I was aware. My unit is looking into it."

"You haven't asked for Five's support."

"I don't need Five's support. Now go away." He held the door open for Lansbury.

"I want an explanation, sir." Lansbury stood his ground. "In fact I demand an explanation."

Lansbury closed the door. Quittenden stood facing him, and Lansbury could see the smug look on that face. White anger built up inside Lansbury. This desk jockey had called him a traitor, deliberately kept him in the cold and dark. And this self-satisfied human computer had not even expressed regret at Vicky Keane's death.

Lansbury's right fist crashed into Quittenden's jaw, knocking him flat. The wine spilt over his evening shirt and blood trickled from the corner of his mouth. Not the best right cross Lansbury had ever thrown, but good enough to floor his opponent. Quittenden look up in disbelief. But he quickly recovered his composure.

"Your're suspended," Quittenden announced.

"Thanks," Lansbury replied, and walked from the room. The Guyanese lady had heard the commotion and Lansbury pointed to the room.

"He's in there, madam, tripped over his ingenious self. Bon appétit."

Lansbury was pleased to be in the open air. He walked to his car and felt relieved. He had wanted to hit Quittenden on one or two occasions. Now he had done it, and he felt good.

Bang goes the pension, he observed, and thought about his wife's reaction.

He did not notice the Renault Fuego parked next to his car with three occupants until two of them got out and confronted him on the pavement. They were very well dressed, hair cropped close, and the first man spoke quietly:

"Evening, D.Ops."

The second man went to Lansbury's own car and opened the rear door.

"If you don't mind, D.Ops." The second man indicated the car's interior. Lansbury's driver was at the wheel. But another man sat on the rear seat, a man with lean features, dark hair, aged about forty. A scar ran down the man's left cheek. In his hand was a pistol, pointed straight at Lansbury.

It was too late to move. The first man was behind him, the second close to his right hand. In any case, Lansbury carried no gun. Who the hell were they?

"Do get in, D.Ops."

They kept referring to him by his official title. He was apprehensive, but did not show them. He sat alongside the man with the gun. Doors slammed. Both cars drove off. The man holding the gun gave it to Lansbury.

"Not loaded," he said, opening a card holder for Lansbury to see an identification inside. It was a blue card, the highest-clearance security pass in the business. There was no name inside the card, just a photograph.

"Who are you? And where are we going?"

"Taking you out of the way for a little while."

170

The man's voice was deep, cultured, but not English. There was a hint of European accent there.

"Don't be put off by the accent. You're not in enemy hands."

Enemy hands was an expression that had gone out with the ark in the Security Services.

"If I don't report back, my office will start looking."

"All taken care of. How was Quittenden?"

Lansbury did not answer.

"Probably as uncommunicative as you."

They drove on, through the London traffic and out onto the Chiswick flyover. The M4 lay ahead. Lansbury had no idea what was happening. His mind raced to provide a solution. The pass was genuine, but the occupants of the car said nothing. They knew who he was, had advised his office. They had to be genuine.

"Who are you with?" Lansbury insisted.

"Richard Lansbury, Director of Operations, M.I.5."

"Very funny."

"What happened with Quittenden?" the man asked.

"I lost my temper," Lansbury replied as the car approached Reading.

"Can he still walk?"

Lansbury nodded. He was perplexed.

"Sorry about your agent, Keane." The man sounded genuine.

"How do you know?"

"Because someone told me. Then you started warfare on the streets. It suits our purpose. Foolish move, though. Where is Wyatt?"

This quiet-sounding, lean-faced man was well informed.

"I don't know. He's very upset about Keane," Lansbury replied, trying to make polite conversation while trying to learn something and give nothing.

"And doubtless going to play soldiers somewhere. Why didn't Quittenden put a leash on him?"

Lansbury shrugged his shoulders.

"It doesn't matter. It really doesn't," the man observed.

Lansbury felt cold and uncomfortable. The man smiled at him. Instead of being reassured, Lansbury was unnerved by it.

"Who are you?" Lansbury asked again.

"You can call me Alpha."

Chapter Twenty-four———————————————

In military terms, we had a tactical withdrawal to Ty Newydd completed at 10:45 P.M. on Monday, August 30.

Even in professional circles, some people think a tactical withdrawal means a retreat. Rome made that mistake at Cannae when Hannibal withdrew his centre. In they went, and the Carthaginian's wings encircled a now committed and entrapped Roman army. Wipe out. The historians tell you that was 216 B.C. and a classic example of one of the six gambits of war. The Saxons made the same mistake at Hastings and spent a lot of time taking extra French.

My move was an old move. But sometimes the old moves are best.

By midnight I had spent an hour in the study, writing specific instructions in several letters. One of them was my will. I had a glass of brandy on the desk and signed the will, put it in an envelope, sealed it with wax, and called Sam.

She came in, looking spectacular in a cheong sam. I avoided the obvious joke and she put her arms around me.

"Don't go," was all she said.

I took her arms away and kissed her forehead lightly.

"Pay attention. In the unlikely event that I have not returned within forty-eight hours, distribute these envelopes to those concerned—Caswell, Johnny, and Mrs. Lewis. If Johnny is not back, his envelope's to be opened by you. Got it? Now scatter."

I don't like saying au revoir to women. They usually howl or become bitchy and recriminating. At least Sam had the good sense to walk out, quietly.

I had dealt the cards, out. Nury al Said had made the phone call to the number he should have called when Lewis had been killed. He was some days late, had my Magnum in his ear, but he got it right. Come bearing two hundred grand or I squeal. Johnny was superintending his second call to give the location, and the time 6:00 A.M., an hour after dawn. Which gave me plenty of time to get there, and left them short of time.

I had the gear on, ready. Magnum and Bowie knife at the waist. Uzi SMG ready to sling round my neck with ten spare magazines in the chest pouch. I dispensed with the balaclava. Instead I had an old camouflage hat which had travelled the world. I smeared my face and the back of my hands with grease; I tied up my bootlaces. Always have tight bootlaces in a gunfight, otherwise your feet contract. You look foolish hopping around.

There was a knock at the door. I presumed Johnny and called, "Come in."

I picked up the shotgun.

"Ready, I—" I turned and saw Ann Lewis. She was standing watching me, dark pools of eyes gazing into mine. Tight black trousers and polo neck sweater started me thinking there were better things to be doing than what I was about to do.

"Hello." I smiled, lighting her cigarette for her.

"I know where you're going. I've been talking to Johnny. May I?" She helped herself to a brandy.

"Sure. That loudmouthed Hungarian will get the sack one of these days."

"I'm coming with you," she announced.

I shook my head.

"I'm dressed in dark clothes," she pointed out.

"Sorry Ann. You'd get your head blown off. I know how you feel. This is down to me. I'm a professional soldier."

"Who are you kidding, man? You were a professional soldier what—over ten years ago?"

"You have been talking to Johnny," I remonstrated.

"Are you trying to expiate David's death, the girl's death, by throwing your own life away? Leave it, Wyatt. Someone will find the people responsible."

"Maybe. In the meantime I'm not waiting around for someone else to be killed."

"You will be." She took hold of my arm. I winked at her.

"I'm indestructible. See you, princess."

I kissed her hand. She looked into my eyes and put both arms around me. She kissed me long, hard and meant it. She let go eventually and I left her in the room.

Outside, the Land Rover was ready. Johnny waited with Detective Chief Superintendent Dan Caswell, who looked at the weaponry.

"Wyatt, rather you than me," he observed. "How many of us are going?"

The question seemed to be prompted by the small number of us outside, three in fact. Nury was in the back of the Land Rover, tied hand and foot, slumbering.

"Just the three of us," I replied.

"What about your lads here?"

"Someone had to mind the shop."

We got in. Caswell in the front, Johnny driving, me in the back.

"How many of them, do you reckon?"

"Not more than eight or ten." Johnny grinned.

I could see Caswell's expression.

"I'm not getting mixed up in this. Come and arrest someone, you said."

"There'll be one or two left to arrest, I expect," I replied.

"And what happens if they get the three of us before we get the ten of them?"

"They win," Johnny joked.

"You two are insane," he muttered, lighting a cigarette.

"Put him out of his misery, Johnny."

"Wyatt goes in. We watch the two approach roads and keep in contact with him by radio. There's a radio in this Land Rover tuned to a police wavelength. Yours. When they're in, and Wyatt gives the signal to you, you call up reinforcements, if you need them. We don't want coppers staked out up there because it's open country. Besides, these boys are good. They're killers. And it'll need the likes of us to stop them."

"And you hope whoever is behind this will be there?"

"Or very close behind," I replied. At least, the way I'd worked it out he should be. If not, we'd have to take a prisoner and try the same trick again. It was not perfect, but it was the only game in town.

"It'll take me over an hour to get any substantial armed force there. Why didn't you tell me before? I know. You didn't trust me."

"Not that, Dan," I replied. "There could have been a leak."

The Land Rover was full of cigarette smoke and the comfortable smell of gun oil. As we drove on, we did not talk. Each of us probably had too much thinking to do. We drove through Llandeilo, the town sleeping, not even the occasional cat moving. Into the country, our headlights played on the road and hedges. The only traffic we encountered was the odd long-distance lorry and a drunk weaving his way homeward. By the old oak tree at Llandovery bridge we turned left. Through the village of Cilycwm and then we were climbing, the Towy swirling below us through rocky clefts.

The sky was clear, cloudless. The stars dotted brightly, clustered brilliantly across the whole sky as far as you could see. There is no sight more calculated to make a man feel mortal and insignificant. We descended through the village of Rhandirmwyn and started climbing toward Llyne Brianne Dam. Occasionally mountain sheep appeared grazing, close to the road.

We passed the lone, lightless farmhouse of Ystradffin and came to the looming mass of the Dinas mountain on our left.

In its valley is a cave reputed to be the hideout of Twm Sion Catti, legendary sixteenth-century Welsh outlaw and anti-Establishment figure. They never told him what was going on, either. I was in good company.

The huge boulder dam was on our left now. I indicated to Johnny to drive up to it, to the edge of the reservoir, so I could look at the spillway and below it water gushing out in a foamy arc to the man-made head of the river Towy.

There was no one about. The crags towered behind me, the dam swept down below me and across the still, silent waters of the shining lake. I could see the hills and the forest. I stood watching everything for as long as it takes to smoke a thin Havana. In the background I could hear Caswell and Johnny talking.

I looked up at the night sky and hoped I would see the next one. If I did not, maybe I would have a new view of the world. But it no longer mattered because the time had come to take up position. Back in the Land Rover we followed the road around the dam, Cefn Farnog and Cefn Coch rising to our right. Johnny and I got out. I saw him, broad-shouldered, grinning through his blackened face, Israeli army beret at the wrong angle, Heckler-Koch in his hand.

"On no account come in," I ordered. "Anything moving down there has to be hostile if I'm going to have a chance. Radio me when you've clocked how many your side. And stay out of sight."

"No point in arguing with you, I suppose?" he asked, resigned to a negative reply.

"No. I have a score to even up for the lady. You understand?"

He nodded. I nodded. We parted silently.

I drove on to the top of the slip road that led down to the water's edge. The hut stood ten yards from the road among the conifers. I stopped the vehicle on the roadway so I wouldn't leave any sign in the earth. We opened the back and hauled out a now-conscious Nury al Said. Caswell lit a Capstan and offered me one.

We stood for a moment gazing at the trees perched on the shale escarpments that jutted out over the water. The air was cold and clean; a light wind was beginning to ripple the lake from the northwest. I looked up again to the sky, the pale yellow moon, and infinitesimal silver of stars.

"Off you go, Dan. Remember, radio in any sightings. If you hear shooting, don't panic. Wait for my signal before calling reinforcements. And if any one unfriendly comes any where near you, get the hell out of here. There's a shotgun and Lee Enfield. Number four in the box in the back. Not to be used, just to make you feel happier. Understood?"

"One thing more." Caswell turned to Said. "I am a police officer. Nury al Said, I arrest you for the murder of David Lewis at Dysant on Wednesday, August twenty-fifth last. I also arrest you for conspiring to murder. You are not obliged to say anything, but anything you do say will be taken down and used in evidence against you."

Said looked puzzled.

"It means you're nicked, son. Don't try and run away."

I led Said to the trees forty yards from the hut. There was a hollow in the ground. I put him down and took his gag off. Then I turned to Caswell.

"You really enjoyed that, didn't you, Dan?"

"Easiest collar I've had in years. See you."

He walked toward the Land Rover, then looked back.

"Be careful, bach. You're a persistent lawbreaker. But life wouldn't be the same without you."

I sat down in the hollow next to Said. He had gambled: instant death if I turned him loose on the streets, or the chance of staying alive if he did as I told him. He'd made the phone calls. Now he was lying there, a cold, frightened, shivering shambles. I hoped that David Lewis, wherever he was, could see the Lebanese now, staked out like a petrified goat that can smell the tiger stalking him.

I lit a cigarette for him and had one myself. We had time for a smoke. He needed one. So did I.

"They will kill you; turn me loose while you can."

"In your condition, chum, you'd last about four hours up here without transport. The wind and the isolation would get you. Pray to Allah I'm the guy who walks away. Without me you're in—" I stumbled for the word.

"Paradise," he replied. I shook my head.

"Not you, chum, not you."

He stayed silent for a while. It was four-thirty. Any moment now and the dawn would come.

"You afraid to die?" he asked.

I quoted the late Winston Churchill.

"I'm prepared to meet my maker. Question being, is he prepared to meet me?"

I hoped today was his day off and the decision would be deferred. Said laughed unpleasantly, so I slapped some tape over his mouth, put a hood over his head, and tied his feet, attaching a nylon cord around the base of the nearest tree. He struggled, uselessly.

"Anything moving gets killed. So be very still and hope the next thing you see is me taking the hood off."

Then I disappeared up to higher ground, so I had a good view of the approaches.

I hoped my choice of the short-range weapons was right. I believed it would have to be that kind of fight. I shoved a round up the spout of the automatic shotgun, and pulled the cocking handle of the Uzi. I could have waited, but the psychological effect was reassuring. I was ready.

Dawn in that high country is a magnificent sight. The sun rose, casting blood-red shadows on cloud over to the east. The wind was cold but clean. I could see for miles around me on two sides. Wild heathland, mountains, trees, the lake shimmering in the early-morning light were sights to remember. At the edge of the lake, high above the wood, a rare kite spiralled upwards, gliding, seeking its prey.

"You and me both," I said to myself.

My watch showed 5:05 A.M. The expectation began to wear on my nerves. I had another hour. A droning sound reached me on the breeze, becoming louder. Then I could hear the whirring of helicopter blades, and high above, from the east, it circled the area and came down.

I cursed myself for thinking car time and not air time. Johnny would be under cover. He'd have made it. But not Caswell. Open ground. Fine for a fight when your opponent is on the level, but airborne—that could be fatal. The wind sounded hollow in my eardrums. The firs swayed gently. Around the descending helicopter the grass flattened in the air turbulence. My heart missed the odd beat or two and my radio crackled. Caswell's voice came over:

"Wyatt, they've got a chopper."

"Dan. Can you find cover?"

"I'm in it, rock outcrop. I'm hidden from the air and I'm armed. But the Land Rover's in the open."

"They can't have more than six up plus the pilot. Five are getting out. Over and out."

Caswell had the sense to hole up away from the vehicle. If the chopper opened fire on the Land Rover, its petrol tank could blow.

"Wyatt—Johnny here. I'm a mile off, at least. I'm coming in."

"Stay put. They might have car backup. Over and out."

Five men ran from the helicopter, fanning out. Their timing was impeccable, synchronized. They wore combat gear. All had submachine guns. And they looked useful, covering each other's approaches, as they came toward the hut, in short rushes.

Suddenly, my one-man ambush was not such a good idea. Five to one was no joke. My mouth felt like sandpaper, and my hands were shaking. There was a void where my stomach should have been. I did not even breathe and prayed Said did not move in the hollow that was on the blind side of the hut.

The five of them closed on the hut, to ten yards, or less, in a semicircle. The chopper took off again, hovering about four hundred yards from me, but I was covered from above by the trees.

Three submachine guns opened up on the hut. The sound

was soul-shattering. Wood splinters flew. I could see three of the five, all within thirty yards. I gripped the shotgun and opened up. I gave no warning; I just fired.

The first two were dead in the air at the same time, spun and smashed by three shots. The third dropped down flat as I fired the fourth time and dirt spurted in his face. He had rolled to his left and the shotgun followed him, my fifth shot making sure of a kill.

I waited now, shotgun empty, Uzi at the ready. I heard the other two moving, caught a flash of movement as one dodged two yards to the base of a tree. The chopper moved in, hovering to see the three dead men, but still above me and out of sight. The noise and the wind were almost unbearable. I had to spot the enemy by movement now, and that advantage soon went because twigs, leaves, anything loose on the ground was sucked into a maelstrom.

I reloaded the shotgun and moved position, slowly, up the slope. The chopper withdrew and everything settled again. But I had lost any idea of my two opponents' position. The deathly quiet was only broken by the distant churning and buzzing of the helicopter.

The odds were better at two to one. Then I heard the chopper come down behind me. It seemed to stay for long enough to let someone out, then was in the air again, circling, high. I reckoned they could carry six plus a pilot. But it could have been eight. The odds were now a possible four to one. And I had been outflanked. Two in front and two behind.

I lay there in a high state of tension. You always think your heart is thumping so loud it can be heard in the next country. It is not, of course. You have to strain eyes and ears for the slightest sound or movement. Your bouncing ventricles and hovering helicopters do not make the task any easier.

The weather had been dry. Movement on the ground should have been easily audible. There was only one of me. I wasn't going to move first. Up front, forty yards away I saw another blur. Then to my left I heard moving sounds. But how far? The guy up front was the decoy. And I realized it too late. He had moved again; I prepared to take a shot at his head as it came round the base of the tree.

A yell split the air as I rolled sideways. A shape flew at me in a shrieking, tumbling mass. I tripped him with my foot. His momentum carried him rolling down the slope. My shotgun had gone off as he knocked it from my grasp with his falling body. A knife had flashed past me. I felt sick and dizzy as I fought to grab the Uzi. A foot had caught me, winding me.

He was on his feet again, fast, pistol in hand. We both fired simultaneously, or so it seemed. A searing pain cut my left arm, but my finger stayed on the trigger and half a magazine of nine-mm Parabellum jerked him like a string puppet gone berserk. He hung lifelessly in midair and rolled down the slope.

The air was full of noise, hissing death, and sucking, whining sounds as the second man fired, on the run, closing distance fast. I rolled to the right and came up shooting, one-handed. The Uzi bucked in my hand. He went down, gurgling, and lay twitching, twenty feet away. Pain like a hundred burning needles shot up my left arm. Blood was spreading into my combat jacket. Vainly I worked the arm but the muscles had gone. Other people's blood spurting around does not bother me. My own, even a pinprick, weakens my resolve.

I had never been hit by a bullet before. The experience was new and unpleasant. Nervous reaction was to lie and throw up. I did not have the time. Gripping the Uzi in the crook of my left arm, I changed the magazine. Then I grabbed the shotgun. I just made the base of a nearby tree as splinters chucked around from another opponent. I was breathing hard. The helicopter roared across. I could see its hull almost directly above me. A blinding flash and bone-shaking explosion filled the air and I was thrown six feet or more. My ears rang as flame started crackling, shooting through the trees.

The bastards were using incendiary bombs of some description.

I crawled away. Another blinding flash. I could hear nothing. The heat sucked in air from all around me. I was choking from lack of oxygen. Suddenly from the ball of flame a man emerged, clothing on fire, gyrating, rolling, a human torch trying to douse itself. I fired the shotgun twice.

God knows how I did it, but I ran on, away from the choking fire, stumbling, hunting cover. Vainly seeking another opponent. The helicopter hovered back, ready to deliver another pattern of fire. I braced myself for it, but the searing fireball never came. The chopper swung away and I thought across to the mountainside behind the woods.

I remembered Said, in the hollow near the hut. But the hut was gone, destroyed. Fanned by the wind, a wall of flame billowed toward me. The choice was simple. Burn to death or run and risk being shot. I ran. I cleared the woods, on to the slip road, coughing, choking, my eyes running tears that blurred my vision. I fell to the ground as bullets ricocheted around me. Through misted vision, I saw the last man running in, firing. He jerked and fell as gunfire came from above the wood. I stumbled into the edge of the road and lay there.

I had not shot him. Who had? Then footsteps. I turned to fire. It would have been too late. I was dead from behind me. A weight landed next to me. Hard breathing sounded. A Heckler-Koch automatic rifle traversed the ground in front of me.

"You've had it rough," Johnny's voice wavered.

"Chopper." I pointed as a helicopter loomed into view, then another. We tried, I thought. Hell, we tried. But they had us. I waited for no sound. The one that gets you, you don't hear.

Through the whirring crash of blades I heard a voice that sounded metallic. Someone was using a loudhailer.

"Wyatt, you old bastard. You all right?"

Johnny was up and waving. The big Sea King helicopters descended to land on the roadway a hundred yards up. Armed men disgorged from the steel bellies, fanning out, S.L.R.s ready. The scene was hazy. Noises disjointed. I must have passed out.

The next thing I remember was an army medic wrapping bandages around my upper left arm. Johnny must have moved me, because we were looking at a blazing forest. Fire engines were arriving. Caswell looked down at me. Johnny gave me a cigarette.

Chapter Twenty-five

The cool, clean breeze brought me back to reality.

"Nick in that arm, sir. Deep furrow where the bullet scored it." The medic stood back. "Be right as rain in a few days."

I nodded, sat up, and tried to stand. My legs were wobbly, so I sat down again. Stretcher parties were coming out of the woods. I ignored everyone and looked at the scenery. Johnny handed me a hip flask. The whisky glowed inside me as I took a very stiff pull.

Richard Lansbury was standing there with a small, square, lean-featured man who had dark glasses and a nasty scar on his left cheek.

"How did you get here, Dick?" I asked.

The other man spoke. "I brought him. We were tracking that helicopter when we picked up a radio signal on a police length that brought us right to it. I think you have Chief Superintendent Caswell to thank for that. The helicopter saw us and made off."

"Just in time," I replied. "Another pattern of fireworks and I'd have been flambéed."

My arm ached. In fact, everything ached.

"Said's dead," Caswell informed me.

"Sorry, Dan."

"Okay. Don't quote me but I'm not heartbroken."

"No big fish," I lamented.

"On the contrary, Major Wyatt," Lansbury's companion

spoke. "They're in the helicopter." He indicated the horizon. "And we know where they are going."

I struggled to my feet. Johnny helped me up, handed me the shotgun, and slung the Uzi round my neck.

"You've had enough." Lansbury put his hand out.

"The hell we have," Johnny growled, seizing Lansbury and pointing him toward the Sea King. I followed. The man in dark glasses made no attempt to stop us. Caswell was not far behind.

We lifted off and Lansbury lit his pipe.

"Where are they going?" I demanded.

"The one bolt hole they have left. To kill Philip Moresby. Out of pure spite."

"They're ahead of us," Johnny observed.

The pilot and his observer were looking at screens and chattering to themselves. Lansbury spoke to the observer and came back to join us.

"Not very far."

"Is Moresby guarded?"

"Yes. But that won't stop them."

I could see a strange expression on Lansbury's mournful spaniel face. And I'll swear that there was a twinkle in his eye.

We landed in the field next to a large house, set back from a minor road in about an acre of ground. The other helicopter was fifty yards away. I gave Caswell the shotgun and told him to watch the other helicopter. Lansbury took the Uzi. I had the only weapon I could really use single-handed—the .357 Magnum.

The house was white, in the style of a turn-of-the-century Boer farmhouse. There was no sign of life—no vehicles, no guards, nothing. We crossed the field, moving fast, and Lansbury lagged behind. Johnny and I leaped the post-and-rail fence simultaneously and hit the ground by some bushes. The house was forty yards in front of us, and twenty to our left was a small stone outbuilding with an open door.

Two men appeared in front of the house, from the porchway. They looked around, each using the pillars of the porch for cover, eyes roving to see movement. One was tall, thin, cadaverous in a black overcoat. Hands in pockets, he watched. The second man was dressed like an American lawyer in a lightweight suit. He was six foot, lean, athletic, with short, fair hair.

We were about to move in when a figure stepped out of the doorway of the outbuilding. He strode deliberately for two or three feet and stopped. He was a pockmarked, one-eyed, pinstriped fool called Sir Philip Moresby, and he had no gun.

"Over here, Q," he called cheekily. "Bring your comrade Svetkin with you."

Quittenden raised a right arm, extended to point at Moresby. Although forty yards away, I could see the pistol in his hand.

The flat bark of a Heckler-Koch sounded as Quittenden's right leg buckled underneath him and he went over. I moved in to cover an unarmed Moresby, but the tall, cadaverous man withdrew a gun from his pocket and fired. Moresby went down.

I dropped to the crouching position and let go at Svetkin. Thirty yards was the range, and he went over with two hollow-point Magnum shells in his chest. Johnny had fired again at the fallen Quittenden, who lay writhing and screaming on the ground.

But Moresby was down. He lay very still. I listened for his heart.

"A nine-mm Makarov won't go through my protective device."

The voice was Moresby's. He sat up and opened a gap in his shirt. "Bulletproof." He smiled.

There was no point in looking at the man Moresby had referred to as Svetkin, but I walked over and saw the grotesque twist of his grey features as he lay in death. Johnny stood over Quittenden, watching the blood ooze from his two shattered kneecaps. Moresby and Lansbury looked on. Quittenden would never walk again. For the rest of his life, whenever he tried to move his legs he would feel pain.

Johnny's face was expressionless as he raised the Heckler-Koch, pointing the muzzle between Quittenden's eyes.

No one moved. Quittenden screamed again:

"Kill me, for God's sake."

Johnny lowered the rifle.

"No way," he replied. "I want you to remember a man you had killed and a girl you betrayed to torture for the rest of your life—and man, I hope you live to be old."

That Hungarian can be a right bastard. But none of us standing there could fault his emotions, or his marksmanship.

Caswell got a car to take us back to Ty Newydd. Something was suspicious about the whole business. But I was tired, shell-shocked, and wounded. Running for that house had finally done me. Moresby told me to call Tuesday afternoon. Then he and Lansbury disappeared in the Sea King. London's urgent and pressing business awaited them.

Caswell had appropriated some scotch from somewhere, and we all had a good pull at it on the way home. I had been right about Quittenden and I owed my confirmation to Vicky Keane. But the fighting was over. Most of us were left alive.

I was back at Ty Newydd by midday. Sam started sobbing with relief; Mrs. Harries insisted on feeding me. I declined. Mrs. Burton was relieved Moresby was safe. I took a walk to the stables, quietly. I was looking for Ann Lewis.

Voices came from the tack room. Siân Lewis was sitting in a corner deep in quiet conversation with young Graham. I was inside before they looked up.

"I told you, Siân." He smiled.

She walked over to me, saw the state of me and my bandaged arm.

"You're hurt."

"I'll live. What did he tell you?"

"He said they couldn't kill you."

I laughed. "Get on with some work, young Graham," I ordered. "Siân, where's your mother?"

"Walking. Over toward the valley, I think."

So I walked, slowly. Over the fields to the valley and the woods. The air was warm and the smell of cordite and burning and death cleared from my nostrils. I could smell the woods, the air, the grass.

A blackbird chattered its warning. I disturbed a grey squirrel. The faint smell of tobacco drifted in the air. I moved quietly and saw Ann Lewis chain-lighting a cigarette. She sat on a fallen tree in a small clearing, wearing the same black outfit she had worn the previous night. I watched her as she shook her head, wiped her eyes with a handkerchief.

"He wouldn't have wanted you to cry. He knew what he was doing," she said aloud.

"He thought he did," I replied.

She came toward me, smiling, laughing, crying, all at the same time.

Chapter Twenty-six————————

My arm still ached. Tuesday, August 31, and the rain was pouring down Whitehall, driven by a fresh wind that gusted against the windows. Sir Philip Moresby poured me a brandy and I sat back in the leather chair.

"While Alpha feels your involvement was prejudicial, I have to tell you I disagree with him," Moresby smiled. "He wasn't the one isolated in Quittenden's custody. And until the opposition had eliminated you, I was safe, although I didn't really feel it at the time. We tend to discount loyalty and friendship in this business. But my God, Wyatt, when Vicky Keane told me she'd had dinner with you, I knew you had not lost your touch. And I felt good. Thank you."

I raised the brandy glass and remembered those who had not made it.

"You're due an explanation, Wyatt, and you may be angry

with me. I didn't enjoy the operation, believe me. But last Monday we had almost finished debriefing the Czech defector when he died on us. They got to him before he came out, slow-acting poison or something. He knew about Quittenden—not his name or position—but he knew we had a highly placed mole. Had he given us specifics, we would have had Quittenden bang to rights before it went any further."

Moresby lit his Havana, then continued:

"Alpha and I were the only parties to the operation. He called me on Monday to check that I'd read the details concerning the Czech's death. I had. Operation Nimrod was the K.G.B. offensive to have me replaced by Quittenden. The idea was years old. But with all this press publicity about superannuated pre-Philby messenger boys, Svetkin must have seen his chance. Moscow Centre would have effectively replaced the P.M.'s security adviser with one of their own. Used sparingly in the future, they would have had a free run forever. Not a new idea, of course. Remember that unfortunate fellow Brandt in Germany—the Chancellor with a Red for a secretary or whatever.

"They set me up using a Libyan, Colonel Abdul Fahd, whom I met on several occasions. I knew Five as watching him. He had information on a matter I'd rather not discuss. We exchanged secrets for money. Centre had set up my bank account with rather more funds than it should have contained. An account, by the way, on which I receive a yearly statement.

"So, I am in custody. Quittenden is in charge of the investigation. Then a very unfortunate coincidence occurs. I see Nigel Appleton, who sees your solicitor for lunch and passes him documents. Obviously Quittenden was worried I might arrange an escape route for my own safety. So they follow Lewis and burgle his office. They find documents relating to you, and lo and behold, you once worked for S.S.D. Quittenden knows Lewis must be removed before he can pass anything to you. We had not expected that, Wyatt, and I must say I deeply regret the civilian casualties in this affair. As you know, I do have a conscience, and one day I suppose I will be called to account for David Lewis and the others over the years. I know the rules say that an individual is expendable when the safety of the state is at risk, but I can never get used to that."

"Why did Quittenden use contract killers?" I asked.

"He was paranoid about using K.G.B. men. Did not want Svetkin to think he'd lost his grip on the operation—or to risk contact. So Lewis is murdered."

"Why not me?"

"Perhaps they were to kill you as well but could not find you in all that countryside. Of course, when you start making waves, Quittenden has problems. He uses his position, quite legitimately, to put the lid on the whole affair. He decides to frame you using Vicky Keane. Unfortunately for him, you turn the tables, so to speak. Quittenden decides to move Mrs. Lewis and daughter to a safe house. He will ostensibly have taken all measures to protect them. Meanwhile, of course, he arranged for his killers to call. By the time his agents arrive there the Lewis women will be dead. He can hold his hand on his heart and say 'My agents were sent to relieve the police guard. It's not my fault they were late arriving.' You were quick off the mark there."

"I expected trouble. Thanks to a very cooperative Caswell I was told the police guard was to be removed. We took out the potential assassins. What then confused me was Quittenden's agents turning up on legitimate business—protection."

"Q is a clever man, and an opportunist. When he discovered Vicky Keane digging up information on the Carl Morgan business and that journalist, he knew his cover was close to being blown. That made the elimination of Nury al Said even more important. Although Said knew Q only as a speaking payola, the fellow was a weak link because of his involvement in the two previous killings. When Said killed Lewis but left witnesses, Said was a dead man. Quittenden then had to meet Svetkin, obtain reliable operatives, and work on poor

Vicky Keane. They used her flat knowing you would go there because you didn't know where else to find her. That's where Q hoped to finish the interference. He could quite legitimately say you and Johnny had beaten the girl to death to extract information. Svetkin's men kill you and depart, leaving Q to come on the scene and claim credit. Yes, a clever man.

"Then, Wyatt, you play the ace. You had Said. Q has another chance and desperately takes it. Alexei Svetkin comes to make sure of finishing the business. They take enough men to the remote area you have chosen, knowing you are behind it, and then it's all over. Dump the bodies in the lake, and say nothing."

"Why did they come after you?" I asked.

"Svetkin knew he was being pursued, that it was all up when Alpha and Lansbury arrived with the cavalry. The idea was to kill me, using Q to gain respectable entry to the safe house, and I'm shot trying to escape. Svetkin diappears smartly and Q says 'I tried.' The last part I don't really know. Desperation, revenge?"

Moresby passed me another brandy. I needed it. The gods had been playing games again and the poor bloody civilians had been expendable. It was all an intellectual exercise to men like Alpha, a mammoth chess game on the board of human weakness and insignificance.

"Of course, the really superb play was to have Moscow Centre offer to exchange an S.I.S. agent for me. I really looked guilty. Then events overtook Alpha's plan and all he did was sit and watch, but not closely enough. Poor Lewis. I suppose his death was the reason for your initial involvement. Why?"

That was a hard question to answer. There were a number of reasons and I was not sure in which order they came. The reasons were maybe mixed up with emotions and values.

"Because a hoodlum shot an unarmed man in cold blood, tried to kill a woman who had seen her husband die. Because the man was going about his lawful business, was on my land, coming to see me. Maybe because I had a guilty conscience about seeing widows and children grieving. Maybe because the reason was me, my past, who I am. Maybe because it was just plain wrong, because things like that should not happen and it's about time someone stopped it."

Moresby sipped his brandy.

"Soldiers," he muttered. "Tough as shield leather and sentimental as Sabine grandmothers. Catullus, or someone. I forget exactly who. Well, the cynics can say what they like, but I know exactly what you mean. By the way, I know it's no compensation, and none of my business, but I did want to satisfy myself that Mrs. Lewis was adequately insured against her husband's death. My department contributed a little something, but I find that Lewis is classed as your employee for insurance purposes which alone will give her a quarter of a million. She is a young woman, Wyatt, and the world is a big place. Time is a great healer—I should know."

I thought about Vicky Keane, but Moresby interrupted me.

"How did you work it all out?"

"Mrs. Burton was the catalyst. Then your note. Then Appleton. Coincidentally, Lewis' death had to be part of a wide picture—Nimrod, as you call it. The four-man tail part of your note was interesting. If whoever was in charge of the operation had only put a four-man tail on an old professional like you, it had to be a setup. So I tried to talk to Lansbury, to make a nuisance of myself, anything to be noticed. You had told me not to trust anyone. And you were right. In my own bumbling way I convinced Vicky Keane I was on the level. My friends located Said, who told me his life story and about two killings with the same modus operandi as Lewis. A nasty specimen named Eustace Souter provided the heavies that were to kill the Lewis women. When Souter told me policemen had called the day after he turned down a contract for his principal, I knew we were in the big league."

I lit a thin Havana. Moresby had been listening very intently.

"Someone had enough influence to call off the police guard

on Mrs. Lewis, to have warned me off via Llewellyn Jones. I expected to be told officially to lay off. Yet as soon as I was warned, the very people the authorities were supposed to protect were in danger."

I paused for a second. Through it all, I kept seeing Vicky Keane.

"Vicky Keane cracked it for me. She talked because she believed me and, I suppose, in you. She gave me Q, even though they had killed her."

I kept hearing her voice. I was holding her and she was dying, again. I must have gone quiet for a minute or two.

"Don't blame yourself, Wyatt." Moresby leaned forward. "It was Alpha's fault, my fault, everybody's fault. But the dice were rolling and we were powerless to stop them. I never thought I would know another Elise. I was wrong. And believe me, Wyatt, Vicky Keane knew what she was up against. Don't insult her memory by feeling sorry for yourself. She would not have wanted that."

He was right, of course.

"It is no consolation, but you evened the score out there on the mountains. Lansbury's reinforcements were surplus to requirements. Only Q and Svetkin were left. By the way, don't plan any holidays behind the Iron Curtain. You killed some of their best men—and Svetkin."

"What happens to Quittenden?" I asked.

"Another coincidence. They were trying to put his knee-caps back together again at the local hospital and he never came around from the anaesthetic. Fortuitous, really. Centre wouldn't accept responsibility for him, and we didn't want him. I have a rotten job, Wyatt, between you and me. Someone has to do it. I do my best. We're still friends, aren't we?"

"Yes, Philip. We're still friends."

Wednesday, September 1, was another blazing day. The picturesque Norman churchyard nestling amongst the oak trees was more suited to wedding photographs than the quiet, dignified, shuffling footsteps of funeral mourners.

I waited till they had gone. All ten of them. Only Dick Lansbury had attended, and that for personal reasons. I took a lonely walk to the far corner of the churchyard, shaded by a hundred-year-old oak tree where a man and a woman stood looking at a fresh grave covered with flowers. They wore black and stood, silently, hopelessly, wondering why. As I walked closer I saw the grey faces lined with age, grief, and tears.

I could feel the eyes watching me as I placed the basket of four dozen red roses at the head of the grave. I stood back and looked, at the blaze of colour against the brown earth, at the stark, square church tower against the blue sky, and at the outlines of the tall oak tree.

I looked at the grave again. The anger had gone, assuaged by the death of too many men on a cold mountain, its traces wiped away when I had put two hollow-point Magnums through Alexei Svetkin. Quittenden was dead. I had finished what Vicky Keane had asked. She lay in the shadow of the oak tree, I hoped in eternal peace.

The empty sensation was still with me. We had been cornered, outmanoeuvred, beaten all ends up, and wasted. The powerful and the mighty had arranged their games, ignored their fallen, and no doubt awaited the chance for another encounter.

The poor, bloody infantry had carried the field, counted their dead, and doubtless waited for the next clarion call to become the human chess pieces in the next intellectual exercise.

I stood back from the grave and told the red-headed lady goodbye and that I did trust her, that I even loved her a little or maybe more than I knew or would allow myself to believe. I told her I would see her again someday. I tried to tell her it had not been for nothing. Yes, the powerful used people, killed them, controlled them, and the people could never win. But you always had to try, to stick in there for what you believe, because the day you stopped trying it would all mean nothing. They could destroy you, but they could not defeat you.

I turned away because the empty feeling was still there. I had gone a step or two when I felt someone touch my arm. The frail middle-aged woman in the black dress and veil had despair etched on the grey yet handsome face.

"Excuse me," she asked, faltering. "Did you know our daughter?"

I nodded. She paused, and continued, as if to excuse herself for approaching me.

"We had not seen her since Christmas. Her work kept her away, but it was important—for the government, I think. Did you . . . ?" Her voice trailed away. She said no more.

"I knew her briefly," I replied. "You should be very proud of her."

I could not say anything else. I was not going to apologize for her death because she had saved my life. She had taken the bastards out with her reflex action. So I walked on through the church gates. I did not look back.

On Friday, September 3, Sir Philip Moresby attended a banquet in the American Embassy in Paris. The Secretary for Defense was on a whistle-stop tour of NATO countries. The President had deemed the European defense situation to be in need of a flag-waving boost by the Alliance's senior partner. His actual words to the Secretary for Defense had been:

"Goddam it, Charlie, get out there and tell the bastards they need our missiles."

Moresby spent some time with th C.I.A. station chief, Paris, over a peripatetic brandy. He did not enjoy Embassy functions. But he needed to make an appearance to scotch the rumours abounding in intelligence circles—that British security had recently suffered some problems, and things were not all they should be. He had squeezed a little quick-drying cement into the brickwork of the special relationship. And he had smiled happily at the Israeli military attaché, giving the man a knowing nod.

He felt a sharp pain in the pit of his stomach, which he put down to indigestion following the gargantuan dinner. The older he got, the more he suffered, and his sixty-third birthday was only a week away. As he circulated, he bumped into the British Ambassador, who spilt brandy over the Secretary's wife. Moresby realized he was unwell. He sat down and summoned a passing waiter to fetch him a glass of water. The Ambassador leaned over him, realizing all was not right. Moresby was breathing hard. Colour drained from his face. He felt his whole body press in on him. Waves of pain lanced his chest. A huge hand seemed to squash him in an unyielding grip. The Ambassador tore Moresby's shirt open. Two Secret Servicemen from the Defense Secretary's entourage discreetly gathered their charge. A third walked over to Moresby. But Moresby was by now unconscious.

A doctor emerged from the consternation. Fifteen minutes later Moresby was stretchered into an ambulance. He died on the way to hospital. Medical diagnosis: Massive coronary thrombosis.

I read about Moresby's death in the Sunday papers. I had that funny feeling at the base of my neck again, the one I get when there is likely to be trouble involving me.

It seemed like a good time to take a fast holiday. I needed one; so did Johnny. Fallon was due in New York later in the week and needed Sam to go with him. I thought it might be a good idea to take the Lewises with us under the circumstances. When I phoned and invited them, Siân answered the telephone and sounded ecstatic at the idea. Her mother did not need a great deal of persuading, which suited me very well. Ann was an attractive girl. And, as Johnny said: "She's more your age than these dolly birds you keep latching on to."

At 11:05 A.M. on Monday, September 6, a dark green chauffeur-driven Rover returned from Downing Street. The two escort vehicles each contained two armed members of the S.A.S. in civilian clothes. The convoy did not stop at the Ministry of Defence in Whitehall, but went instead to an address in Lancaster Gate.

Gareth Llewellyn Jones stepped out of the Rover, smiled at his chauffeur, and walked briskly up the steps of the Georgian house. The black door opened automatically and he walked in, across a marble-floored hallway where a sergeant in Royal Marines uniform rose from behind a desk and saluted him.

Llewellyn Jones continued through the hallway to a door on his left, observed continually by closed-circuit television. He entered the room, shut the door behind him, and hung his coat on a stand behind the door. He smiled at the severe middle-aged woman who wished him good morning, and pressed a button on the console at the side of her desk.

A wall partition slid open. He walked through into another room, soundproofed, windowless, its walls decorated with computer screens, television, electronic maps, and diagrams. The room contained a single desk, chair, and an armchair. Llewellyn Jones sat back in the chair and surveyed his new office.

The Prime Minister had congratulated him on his new appointment.

He congratulated himself that he did not have any shares in Aberinvest Corporation. News was that an executive jet en route to the United States had disappeared. It was reported that the passengers had been Messrs. Wyatt, Peter Fallon, a Hungarian named Jan Szczelskowski, a secretary, and two women named Lewis.

He lit a cigarette and smiled. The first part of his brief from Moscow Centre had been carried out. The second part was to change the Prime Ministerial mind concerning the location of certain missiles.

I imagined whoever had put the bomb aboard the plane would presume we had exploded over the North Atlantic. The American Coastguard Service did likewise, and if they ever catch up with me for the bill for the search—well the point is, if someone really wants to get you, the world is too small a place to hide.

But if no one is looking for you, Canada is quite an acceptable place to be. No one knew we were there. I needed a few

months' peace and quiet. And when I surfaced again, I'd be making a few discreet enquiries.